Beers
Tapped Out

D1452094

Also by P.M. LaRose

Beers Abroad
Beers Ahead
Bet on Beers
First Case of Beers

Beers
Tapped Out

Trouble Every Day

P.M. LaRose

liquid
rabbit
publishing

This book is a work of fiction. The names, characters, and incidents are products of the writer's imagination or have been used fictitiously and are not to be construed as real. Any resemblance to persons, living or dead, actual events, or organizations is entirely coincidental and too bizarre to take seriously.

Cover design and illustration by P.M. LaRose

Liquid Rabbit Publishing
2010 Glasgow Ave.
Baton Rouge, LA 70808

pmlarose.com
email: BeersAhead@gmail.com
Facebook: PM LaRose
Facebook: Beers Detective Agency

ISBN 978-1-7324951-7-3

First Edition: October 2020
10 9 8 7 6 5 4 3 2 1

For Gina Marie and Michael

No way to delay
That trouble coming every day

—Frank Zappa

La Scala Minneapolis

9 Executive Offices

8 Bedding · Men's Shoes · Luggage

7 Break Room · Kitchenware

6 Men's Dept. · Seasonal Gifts · Candy Counter

5 Purses · Jewelry · Watches

4 Electronics · Appliances · Returns

3 Casual Wear · Women's Foundations

2 Women's Shoes · Fashion Wear

1 Sportswear · Cosmetics

B Deli · Sporting Goods · Maint.

Prologue

A bullet to the heart is a good indicator the victim died of non-natural causes. In this case, it was the first true murder in the department store where I worked, and it hit very close to home.

Most employees concluded terrorists had struck in the heart of the Twin Cities. After all, this was just days after planes had crashed into the Twin Towers in New York City, bringing the threat, and reality, of terrorism to American shores.

It was during an inventory reduction sale at La Scala Minneapolis. In the retail biz, inventory reduction usually means the store's buyers screwed up and overstocked unwanted goods. In this case, my job got real busy. You see, I'm head of security for this place of commerce.

Too many folks, mostly kids, had been taking to heart the inventory reduction part of the plan and leaving out the sale. Shoplifting went up at an alarming rate, and I was constantly up and down the 10 floors of the department store in a quest to nab five-finger discounters.

We call that a Code 32. Shoplifters are a sad fact of life in the retail industry. They're taken into account when prices are affixed to goods and play all sorts of havoc when inventory is conducted quarterly.

I was dealing with the latest Code 32 in menswear when the call came in. A dead body is never an easy sight to behold. In my short term in the department store trade, however, I had become all too familiar with that scenario—in Las Vegas, in London and even here in Minneapolis, headquarters of the La Scala empire.

This body, however, shocked me to the core because I was personally involved. Those other victims were people I didn't really know very well. This one constituted a family affair, in more ways than one.

1

Friday, September 14, 2001

Nine-eleven was more than a date. It was the day everything changed, from the mundane cares of everyday existence to a pervasive feeling of unease, a sense that life would never be the same again.

It was a feeling of insecurity.

For someone whose job title includes the word security, I can tell you it was worse than the worst dread I could imagine.

Let me provide a little background so you get the full picture. My name is James A. Biersovich, Beers for short. After working as a reporter for years, I got fed up and quit my job at the Minnesota Herald. A vice president at La Scala, Jane Mertin, needed a new security assistant and offered me a job. I took it.

That was two years ago. I no longer work for Jane, but my girlfriend, Emmie, does. Or did. More on that later.

Due to my innate knack for figuring out whodunits—my friends say it's more like sheer luck—I have been promoted several times by the owner of the La Scala chain, Johnny Scalabrino. He has taken me under his wing and groomed me to be his troubleshooter, a task for which I am totally unqualified, in my mind. Whenever there's a crime to solve, and lately that has involved murder far too often, he points me at it and kicks me in the rear end. Go fix it, he says.

I don't like being around dead bodies. If that were appealing to me, I would work at a funeral home. My repeated attempts to exit this position have been thwarted, however, by a very persuasive argument: money. Scalabrino keeps upping the ante, making it tough to walk away. Besides, I still haven't figured out what I want to be when I grow up.

Complicating the matter is the fact that my gorgeous girlfriend works just down the corridor. Any time I want I can pop into her office and see that pretty face, knockout figure and deep emerald eyes. The emerald eyes of Emerald "Emmie" Slayton. That perk alone is sufficient. Throw in the bread and it's impossible to leave.

Did I mention the complications? OK, here goes. Emmie serves as Jane Mertin's secretary, which can be a bit awkward. But that doesn't hold a candle to the fact that Jane is also my dad's girlfriend. You can't imagine the trepidation that has caused me.

I kept thinking something's gotta give in this whole setup. Unfortunately, something did.

ON THE DAY in question, like I say, everyone was still in a state of suspended animation. Automatons going about their work without consciously thinking about anything other than the suddenly perilous state of everyone's existence.

I was in the throes of drafting a new security plan to take into account this strange new world thrust upon us. Scalabrino had asked for my thoughts on how to conduct business while keeping employees and customers safe and doing so unobtrusively.

My first thought was: "Can't be done." Then I assembled the brain trust to give it a second thought.

The brain trust consists of myself and my part-time assistants, Lena Fangeaux and Tina McEntire. Lena is stationed on the fifth floor, where she's one of the top jewelry saleswomen. Lena has the technical brain I'm lacking. She does all my computer research. Although I have an extra desk in my office for her to occupy, she's rarely there. The commissions on jewelry are just too lucrative.

Tina works in cosmetics on the first floor. She is the streetwise segment of the triumvirate. Her forte is gathering intelligence through direct conversation and piecing together clues from the grapevine. She also has contacts in the police department.

So you're wondering what my role is in this kitchen cabinet. Well, I'm the one who has to figure out the final solution by fitting together the various pieces of the puzzle. So far, I have managed to do that by intuition or stroke of luck. It's some kind of magical gift, I think. I've tried applying logic to the strange cases I've been confronted with, but that doesn't seem to work. I just have to wait for that bolt out of the blue to spark the answer. Usually, there's music involved, for some reason.

Anyway, I called Tina and Lena up to my office on the ninth floor to get their thoughts on securing the property to prevent a terrorist attack. Tina, ever the smartass, wanted to know whether the budget for our little project would include the cost of an anti-missile defense system. Or maybe a titanium bubble capable of deflecting a 747.

"Within reason," I replied. "We need to come up with a plan that will take into account the most likely sorts of events. A plane or missile hitting the building is highly unlikely."

"Dat's what dey thought in New Yawk," Lena replied. If I haven't mentioned it, Lena has a bit of an accent. She's from New Orleans.

"So what are you saying—body scanners, barriers to prevent someone from driving a van full of explosives through the front of the store...?" Tina asked.

"Possibly," I said. "That's the kind of thing that could be done if the cost were feasible. And, of course, if it didn't impinge on sales."

"Of course," Tina retorted. "Safety first—right after revenue."

Lena cackled.

"The biggest security system is already in place," Tina quipped. "That big hole in the street." She was referring to a current sewerage repair project that had resulted in the roadway directly in front of La Scala being excavated, causing all sorts of traffic mayhem and making it harder for customers to reach the store.

"Just think about it over the weekend and get back to me Monday with whatever ideas you come up with. We'll make a list and put them in order of biggest bang for the buck. Sorry, bad metaphor."

"How ya gonna know dat? We gotta figyah out da cost?" Lena asked.

"No, just what our common sense tells us."

"Well, we'd better let you get on it," Tina said, rising to go. "You're going to need all the time you can get just to come up with that common sense stuff." She left, followed soon after by Lena, chuckling as she went.

Tina was right, of course. At the moment there was no making sense of anything, common or not.

THE CONSTRUCTION PROJECT—or should I say *obstruction* project—directly in front of the store was a huge headache. The epidermis of the street had been scraped off, and workers were now jackhammering through the roadbed. A shed was perched at the edge of the developing crater. Traffic on Hennepin Avenue had been diverted to a single lane each way through the thoroughfare, a nightmare for commuters.

Salmon Foster, the CFO of La Scala Minneapolis, had sent me to find out what was going on, since apparently no one had notified the store about the plan, and it seemed to be presenting logistical problems for customers.

I approached a group of workers standing outside the construction shed.

"Excuse me, gentlemen. Can you tell me what's going on here?"

A burly guy with "Greek" embroidered on his shirt scowled at me and said, "Sewer work."

The explanation was lacking some details, so I pressed further. "I see. And how long is this going to take?"

Another guy spoke up. "Couple of weeks. Now, if you'll excuse us…" His name was Footie.

"But if you could just—"

Yet a third guy turned and took me by the arm. "You need to leave. This is a construction zone. Hard hats only." I could see his nametag: Steel. None of these fellows seemed to have real names. Foster was going to blow a gasket when I told him I was brushed off by Greek, Footie and Steel.

2

Prior to that infamous date of 9/11, I just thought my job was complicated. My mission as head of security for the La Scala chain—Italian-themed department stores in Minneapolis, Chicago, Las Vegas and San Francisco—involved overseeing all manner of issues regarding integrity of the buildings and merchandise.

I had fought with Johnny Scalabrino about installing cameras in the stores and won. It wasn't easy. He resisted for a long time due to an incident involving security cameras years earlier, one that caused him no end of embarrassment and harassment from his old man.

But my winning argument was twofold: His stores were easy targets without cameras, and I would resign unless they were installed.

Believe me, I had been trying to resign almost as long as I had been employed there. Scalabrino kept making it harder and harder, however, by continually hiking my pay. And, of course, providing a cushy job for my girlfriend when she wanted nothing to do with the place anymore.

If only I could turn back the hands of time...

Everyone wants to do that, I'm sure. We all want more time, another chance to get it right. But time moves forward and so must we, dealing with daily issues ranging from the mundane—Code 32s—to the catastrophic. Like 9/11.

It was only three days after that fateful date, when the shock was still fresh in everyone's mind, that murder made its debut at La Scala in downtown Minneapolis.

The question that immediately came to mind was: Is this part of the terrorism that invaded America? A reasonable question at the time.

This had never happened at La Scala. Just as 9/11 had never happened to America, and then it did. That they occurred in the same week left many people too stunned to function. On my rounds through the store in the days following that national tragedy, the sight of a clerk numbly gazing off into space became commonplace. Even the customers looked like they were going through the motions.

Of course, traffic was down due to that event and the street work blocking half of Hennepin Avenue in front of the store. The ensuing logjam was a huge pain in the ass, and most folks didn't want to fight that.

THE MORNING of the murder, my buddy Freddie called. He sounded disturbed. The general malaise apparently had infected his usual carefree mood. Freddie is a reporter friend from my days in the newspaper world.

"I'm thinking about entering phase three," Freddie said.

"Phase three? What is that?"

"Well, you know how you're a kid and go to school for years? That's phase one. Then you grow up, get a job and work for years? That's phase two."

"I never heard about these phases."

"Well, I'm telling you now."

"So what's phase three? Abducted by aliens?"

"Get serious, Beers. Phase three is your life after work."

"You mean retirement?"

"Well...not exactly."

"That's what it sounds like to me. Exactly. You want to retire, Freddie?"

"No. Just move on to the post-working phase."

"So be a bum, in other words."

"Beers, you're not taking this seriously."

His tone indicated he wasn't kidding. I felt somewhat chastised.

"OK. What's going on, Freddie? You having a mid-life crisis? Damn, you're only, what, thirty-five?"

"Thirty-seven. And no, it's not that. I've just been rethinking things. Wondering if I'm on the right path. There's got to be more to life."

"Freddie, that's the classic mid-life crisis. I should know. Been there, done that."

"So what did you do?"

"Duh. Hello? Look where I work now."

"Oh. Right."

"Freddie, just don't do anything drastic."

"Beers, I'm not impulsive. I'm not gonna jump off a bridge or blow my brains out."

"That wasn't what I was thinking, Fredster."

"I've gotta go. I'm supposed to meet this chick at The Crater."

"Chick?"

"P.R. for the Wild. Just hired. Told her we needed some background on the new starting lineup for the upcoming season."

"So she's cute."

"Knockout. Tits like you wouldn't believe—"

"I get the picture. Call me in a few days after the dust settles. Better yet, I'll call you. Just, like I say, don't do anything you'll later regret."

"Beers, everything I do I later regret."

We hung up, and I started worrying that the Freddie I knew and mostly tolerated would turn into a completely different person as a result of current events.

Then I thought maybe that wasn't such a bad thing.

And I felt bad about thinking that.

3

It was getting on toward noon on that fateful day. I know this because I made note of it, as I do most things. The memory isn't what it used to be, and even then it wasn't.

The notepad I use is the same kind Freddie carries around. It's a holdover from my days on the minor sports beat. Names, places, dates, quotes, impressions—they all go into the notepad for future reference.

Shortly before the hour and minute hands met at number 12, Emmie came into my office. Usually it's the other way around, but that morning she had been to the dentist, always a nerve-wracking experience. Not that she has bad teeth. It's just that teeth in general need a lot of maintenance because they get a daily workout.

In this instance Emmie had a cavity that needed filling, and it took most of the morning. Her mouth was still a little numb, but she managed to give me a quick peck on the lips before heading down to the executive suite. She was skipping lunch, since she came in late, so I was on my own.

As I started to leave my office, I heard a goose-bump-inducing scream from down the corridor. I ran that way. A crowd was already gathered at the door to Emmie's office, which led into Jane's inner office.

Pushing my way through, I spotted Jane in her high-back leather chair, with a large red blotch in the middle of her white blouse. Her head was thrown back, and her eyes were staring at a spot on the ceiling. I didn't need to take her pulse to know that she was dead. Emmie lay sprawled on the floor in front of Jane's desk.

"What happened?" I yelled to the crowd at large. I bent over Emmie to see if she was OK.

"Step aside!" I heard a voice bellow. It was Salmon Foster, the de facto head of operations at La Scala Minneapolis. "What's the commotion?"

He walked behind the desk to get closer to Jane. "Very funny, Jane," he said, "but Halloween is six weeks off." Then I saw him grab Jane's arm and quickly recoil in horror. The crowd was murmuring.

"Clear the room! And not a word of this!" he yelled. As the crowd dispersed, he looked down and saw me attending to Emmie. "Biersovich! Call an ambulance! And get a guard up here!" Then he left.

I managed to get Emmie to her feet and walked her out to her desk, closing the door to Jane's office. Then I dialed for an ambulance and called down for the First Sentinel rent-a-guard on duty.

"Wha...what happened?" Emmie said with a glazed look.

"You fainted," I said. "Just rest. When you feel better, we'll go down to my office."

"Jane...is she...?" Emmie began tearing up.

"Don't know. Ambulance on the way," I replied.

Then she did a full-on blubber. I held her shoulder and let her cry for a minute. When the guard arrived, I stationed him at the outer door, took Emmie down to my office and closed the door. Emmie continued crying out of control, so I had no choice but to wait it out.

I made a call to Scalabrino's mansion to deliver the bad news. No one answered, so I left a vague message reporting a problem at the store. I wasn't sure which code to report.

When the ambulance arrived, the guard called and asked me to return to the executive suite. One of the paramedics was waiting in Emmie's office; the inner door remained closed.

"You found the body?" he asked. The guy had a name tag that said Frenchie.

"No, the secretary did. I'm Jim Biersovich, in charge of building security."

"OK. Well, we've summoned the coroner and alerted the police." Just then the inner door opened and two paramedics exited, toting satchels. I could see Jane still perched in her chair like she was waiting for Foster to barge in and start giving her orders.

"So she's dead," I said.

"Afraid so," Frenchie replied. "I think we need to keep everyone out of here, since it's a crime scene. But the detective will tell you what to do. We should wait out there," he said, pointing to the lobby of the executive suite.

While we awaited arrival of the crime tech team, executives and their secretaries peeked out of their doorways. Their expressions were a mixture of concern, dread and numbing fear, and I could do nothing to reassure them.

A group of plainclothes policemen and a medical examiner arrived at the scene. The guy in charge chatted with the paramedics for a minute, then asked my name. He introduced himself as Detective Charles Farraday. Then they entered the inner office and closed the door behind them.

Five long minutes passed. Then Farraday emerged and told the paramedics they could leave. He motioned me aside and asked whether there was a place he could interview staff privately. I showed him to the executive conference room.

"We need to secure the floor," Farraday said. "No one enters or leaves. Can you station a guard at the elevator?"

"Sure," I said. The guard was right behind me when I turned around, so he heard everything. He headed to the elevator lobby.

"Get me a list of everyone who works up here," Farraday ordered. "Then bring it to me in the conference room. Can you do that?"

"Sure," I said.

"Now, who found the body?"

"That would be Emmie. Jane's secretary."

"Where is this Emmie?"

"I'll get her." He smiled and pulled out a cell phone while he headed into the conference room and closed the door.

Before getting Emmie, I thought it best to brief the boss on the situation. So I went into Foster's office to deliver the bad news. I learned long ago that it didn't pay to keep him in the dark a second longer than necessary.

Foster's secretary, Candace, told me he was on a call and couldn't be bothered. I told her he could call me, and I'd update him on events.

Since I needed the names of everyone who worked on the ninth floor, I popped into personnel and asked the secretary to prepare a list. Then I headed down to my office.

No Emmie.

I dialed her cell phone, but she didn't answer. Perhaps she was in the ladies' room. Understandable, given the circumstances.

4

It didn't take long for Tina to call me. I've described in previous reports how she has this uncanny knack of finding out about happenings faster than almost anyone else. In this case, she tried to come up to the ninth floor but was turned back by the guard at the elevator.

"You need to tell me exactly what's happening now," Tina demanded.

"Still too early to tell. I have to go talk with a detective," I said.

"Someone's dead."

"I'll call you when I can," I replied. I hung up before she could give me the third degree. Re-entering the executive suite, I asked one of the secretaries to check the ladies' room. A small group was standing outside the conference room, waiting to be summoned to the inner portal.

Farraday opened the door, looked around, then wagged his finger at me. I approached.

"Who's in charge here?" he asked.

"That would be Mr. Foster. Salmon Foster. He's the CFO."

"Get him," Farraday said, closing the door in my face.

When I returned to Foster's secretary's office, she motioned me into the inner sanctum. Foster was staring out the window onto Hennepin Avenue, glass in hand. It looked like a straight shot of scotch. He took a swig, then spoke.

"Biersovich, do you know how long I've worked in this business?"

It sounded like a trick question, so I was reluctant to guess. "No idea, sir."

"Twenty-four years," he answered. "I've been working in retail for over two decades. I started out as a shoe salesman at Macy's in New York. You could get a fine pair of shoes for thirty bucks. Nowadays, you can barely buy the laces for that."

He paused and took another sip, then turned around to address me.

"We didn't need security tags or guards in the store. People were mostly law-abiding. Sure, there were a few shoplifters, always have been. But nobody came into a department store with a gun and pistol-whipped a clerk." He was referring to an incident earlier that year in which armed robbers hit La Scala.

"No, sir," I said, just to test my vocal cords.

"Those days are gone," he continued. "It's a sad fact of life that we need guards and cameras to protect the store and customers. I don't like it. I don't like it one bit." He finished off his drink and set the glass down on his desk.

This seemed to be my opening. "Mr. Foster, Jane is dead." He didn't speak, just sighed heavily. "There's a detective here. He wants to speak with you."

"Send him in."

"Sir, he wants you to meet with him in the conference room."

Foster grimaced and walked past me. "Candace, I'll be in the conference room," he said. He left, and Candace turned a worried expression to me.

"Routine," I said, then followed him out.

I could hear a commotion in the elevator lobby, so quickly went that way to see what was going on. The guard had both arms propped against the open elevator door and was arguing with someone trying to get off on nine.

"It's closed for now," the guard was saying.

"Move your arms or lose them!" I heard a familiar voice bellow. I didn't have to see the face to know it was Joseph Terrazzo, otherwise known as Joe T, Scalabrino's cousin and right-hand man.

"It's OK," I told the guard, easing his arm out of the way. Joe T exited the elevator with a long stare at the guard, then pulled me down the hall away from the executive suite.

"Spill it," he said.

"Looks like someone was killed. Homicide," I replied.

"Who?"

"Jane Mertin. Vice president of facilities. She was found in her office with some sort of chest wound. Like maybe someone shot her."

"Not Foster? Too bad."

I let that comment slide.

"There's a police detective here, Farraday. He's interviewing people in the conference room. Foster's in there now."

"Let's go." He led me down the hall to the executive offices, told me to wait, knocked on the conference room door and entered without waiting for permission. He closed the door, and loud arguing ensued.

When the door reopened, Foster emerged, followed by Joe T, who took my arm and dragged me back down the hall to my office. Foster sat at the spare desk where Lena sometimes works, and Joe T closed the door.

"Tell me everything you know," he said.

I proceeded to tell them what little information I had, including the current unknown whereabouts of Emmie. They encouraged me to locate her and find out what she knew before she talked with the detective. No explanation why.

"This is a very sensitive matter," Foster said unnecessarily.

"After you talk to the detective, come to the mansion," Joe T said. "Johnny will be waiting." He left, followed by Foster. I returned to the executive suite to await my turn in the grilling room.

5

mmie still hadn't shown up, and I was getting worried. The secretary I asked to check the ladies' room didn't see her. I wondered whether Emmie had left the store during the commotion, before the detective arrived. She wasn't answering her cell phone, so I was in the dark.

Farraday soon summoned me to chat. He knew the identity of the deceased but not much else. He wanted leads to a motive for the unknown perpetrator. He asked for the list of ninth-floor employees. I said personnel was working on it.

"Where is the secretary? I need to speak with her next," he said.

"I don't know. Emmie isn't answering her phone."

"Tell me about Emmie."

"Emerald Slayton, Jane's secretary. She had just come back from a dental appointment when she found...the body."

"So why did she leave after that? And where did she go?"

"I found her on the floor. She had fainted. I took her down to my office, down the corridor there. She was pretty shaken up."

"And you left here there? Alone?"

"Yes, sir. Like I say, she was in shock."

"You're the head of security, you said?" he asked.

"Yes, sir."

"And you just left the victim to attend to Emmie. You didn't check to see if she was still alive or call an ambulance..."

"Well...it was obvious..."

"You just assumed she was dead."

I didn't like his accusation. "Sir, with all due respect, I've seen dead bodies before. Murder victims. And I did call an ambulance."

"What did you do after you found Emmie on the floor?"

"She had fainted, so I helped her up and walked her out to her desk. She became hysterical, so I brought her down to my office so she could calm down away from the scene."

"Then you just left the main witness alone, and now she's disappeared." He frowned at me. "Did you touch anything in the office?"

I shook my head.

Farraday pulled a plastic bag from his jacket pocket and pushed it toward me. In it was a crumpled Post-it that said: "Back around noon Fri."

"Have any idea what this is? We found it in the trash."

"Like I say, Emmie was at the dentist this morning. She must have left this note for Jane. Probably put it on the door before leaving for the day yesterday. Then Jane took it off when she arrived and threw it away. I'm guessing."

"So the door was closed."

"I would imagine."

"We don't guess or imagine in this business," he retorted. "We ascertain the facts. We need this secretary to do that. You lost her, so go find her."

That was my rude dismissal. I had been acquainted with this detective for only a short while but already didn't like him.

IT TOOK A FEW MINUTES to talk my way past the guard I had stationed at the elevator. I managed to convince him that Johnny Scalabrino wasn't one to keep waiting.

On the way out, I stopped to speak with Tina at the cosmetics counter on the first floor. No, she hadn't seen Emmie leave the store. Somehow, Tina knew there was a murder and that the victim was a "suit." Her grapevine shortwave was picking up strong signals again. I refused to elaborate and headed to the parking garage.

Scalabrino's mansion on the parkway south of downtown Minneapolis was as I recalled it from previous visits: ornate, comfortable, reeking of big money. The boss was knocking balls around on the blue felt pool table in his enormous office/den when I arrived. His minions apparently were out and about.

"Report," he commanded, without looking up.

"There has been a death at the store," I began.

"I know that. I know it's Jane Mertin. Tell me something I don't know."

Joe T had obviously filled in the essential information.

"We have no idea when it happened or who did it. A Detective Farraday is interviewing the staff on the ninth floor."

"Go on."

"The body was found by Jane's secretary, Emmie Slayton. She's MIA at the moment. That's all I know."

"Where is Foster on this?"

"Beg pardon?"

"Has he got a handle on it? I want a lid kept on this until we know what happened."

"I suppose he has it under control. He was the first person interviewed."

"Be available for Detective Cuccia this afternoon," he said, waving his cue and resuming his pool playing. It was also a cue that I was dismissed.

On the way back downtown, I wondered what role Cuccia would play in the investigation. In my former dealings with him, it seemed he was somehow part of Scalabrino's posse, his man on the inside of the police department. With a different detective in charge of the case, one presumably not on Scalabrino's payroll, control of the situation would be trickier. And I knew Johnny Scalabrino was all about control. He called the shots, and no second-guessing was allowed. Even his cousin, Joe T, tiptoed lightly around him.

I detoured toward Emmie's apartment in Uptown. Since she wasn't answering her phone, I figured she had gone home and taken a nap, or perhaps started drinking. With a key to her apartment, a perk of our intimate relationship, I could check up on her.

Unfortunately, there was no sign of Emmie. If she had returned to her apartment, she had already left. Perhaps she was back at work and taking her turn in the grilling room. I hoped that was the case because I was getting worried about her.

6

Word had traveled throughout the store by the time I returned. They had seen the coroner's office roll out a draped gurney. Somber faces assisted customers at every counter. Tina was doing a woman's nails with a stunned expression and didn't even look up when I passed.

The elevator was unguarded, and detectives had departed when I arrived back at the executive offices. Still no sign of Emmie, however. The door to Foster's office was closed. He apparently was huddling with the other suits.

My office door was locked when I tried the handle, giving me hope that Emmie had returned and holed up in there. I knocked, and Lena opened the door.

"Get yaself in heah, Beers. We got work ta do," she said.

"Have you seen Emmie?" I asked.

"Naw. Duhtectives crawlin' da place right now. Mebbe on dah sixth floah."

"I need to find her. She was the one who found Jane."

"So she's really toes up?"

I nodded.

"Fostah pulled me outta jewry when he couldn't find ya." I knew that meant something important. Dragging Lena away from the jewelry counter was serious business.

"What did he tell you?"

"Dat he wants ta stawt beefin' up security now. Like *right* now."

"More guards?"

Lena nodded. Getting First Sentinel to send more hired guards to the store was an extra expense but seemed fairly easy to do.

"Get dose camrahs installed." Although Scalabrino had finally acquiesced to my demands for security cameras, the legal department was dragging its heels on giving its blessing.

"OK. What else?"

"Metal detectah."

"Are you kidding?"

She shook her head.

"That's crazy! We might as well put up a closed sign. Customers won't go for it."

"You tell Fostah dat," she replied.

Reasoning with Foster would be impossible. Unless...

"I'll make him see the light," I said. "Meanwhile, are you assigned to me?"

Lena nodded again.

"OK. I need you to do some research." Lena was a whiz in the cyber world and could find out just about anything I requested. But we would need some assistance from Tina also, so I rang her extension. Her somber mood brightened when I told her what I needed. She said she would get right on it.

And I had some legwork to perform myself. Time to get it in gear.

"NO, HAVEN'T heard from her."

Gidget was no help but I had to give her a try. As a past roommate of Emmie, I knew she still kept in touch, although I had no idea how often. But Emmie apparently didn't seek out Gidget when she went AWOL.

After that, I had little clue as to where to look. Emmie ran with a younger crowd when we weren't together. The age difference—almost a two-decade gap—complicated matters.

Her parents lived somewhere around Indianapolis, she once told me. Our relationship hadn't advanced to the point where she took me to meet her folks, however. But if anyone could locate them, it would be Lena.

Emmie also had two siblings, but I had no idea where they lived. Again, Lena would have to come through with the details.

Tina wasted no time getting back to me with information. Her contact within the police department, a patrolman she worked with closely during her short stint as a uniformed officer, said the initial focus of the investigation was on Salmon Foster and the other executives. She could not get any details on why.

Police were ruling out any possible terrorist links, she said, due to the fact that the murder weapon, a .22-caliber pistol, wasn't considered a normal tool for Mideastern types. She had been shot once in the heart and once in the right foot.

As for Jane Mertin, I knew very little about her private life outside of her dating my father. I really didn't want to know. I had met one of her sons around Christmastime but had no idea how to get in touch with him. Perhaps the police were already on that. And the other son, wherever he might be.

With a call to First Sentinel, I lined up three more guards to patrol the store. I made sure to inform Joe T, just in case there was an issue. There wasn't. He vetoed Foster's notion of metal detectors, however, saying not only would it be impractical, the big boss wouldn't go for it. He said he would grease the skids for the security camera project.

Joe T wasn't surprised to hear Foster was a suspect because he had heard rumblings from board members. He couldn't reveal anything at the moment but would inform me in time.

The afternoon wore on with little new information arriving. Just about quitting time, however, the detective strolled into my office and shut the door.

"Biersovich."

"Detective Farraday."

"Where's your witness?" he asked with a steely glare.

"Can't locate her."

He considered that a moment. "It's very important that we speak with her. She's not a suspect at this juncture but her absence...well, that doesn't look good."

"There is no way she's involved, sir. I know Miss Slayton very well. I can assure you she had nothing to do with this."

"Be that as it may, I need to speak with her. What information do you have?"

I gave him what little I knew of her family and former roommate, along with her current address and phone number.

"Her brother is under house arrest." His statement hit me like a ball-peen hammer. "Did you know that?"

"No, I...I don't know anything about her brother."

"Her personnel file is quite interesting. I assume you've perused it."

As a matter of fact I hadn't, but I didn't want to admit that since it was my job to know stuff, being head of security.

"What part do you find interesting?" I asked. A shot in the dark to see whether he would clue me in. He wouldn't.

"I'll be in touch." He exited, and I was left to ponder the hidden skeletons in Emmie's closet. Even I could figure out it was time to really start worrying.

7

O f course, there's always another shoe to drop in the department store biz. It came when I walked into my high-rise apartment overlooking downtown Minneapolis.

I didn't expect to find Emmie there waiting for me, although my heart rate jumped as I was unlocking the door and heard a muffled voice within. It turned out to be Dad on the answering machine, leaving his fourth message. I replayed it and the other three just to make sure I was hearing correctly. He was at the police station being questioned.

After a quick circuit of my place to make sure Emmie hadn't been there and left a note, I motored down to the cop shop. Dad was "assisting" authorities at the moment, and I had to just wait. So I found a suitably uncomfortable chair and parked in it.

While waiting for him to emerge, I called Tina and asked whether her police contacts could provide any more information. She already knew about Pops being grilled, naturally, and said authorities were trying to locate Jane's ex-husband. That seemed a more likely venue of inquiry because it was seemingly always the spouse or ex-spouse who committed a murder, at least in TV shows.

Knowing my father as well as I did, I could have told police there was no way he was capable of murder. He was too easygoing, upbeat, a real pussycat. They must be trying to discover any possible association with someone who wasn't so copacetic with Jane.

Forty-five minutes after my arrival, Dad emerged. He had a grim expression and said he could go now. Outside the station, he told me they had treated him like a suspect. I assured him that was probably routine. He also said he was advised not to leave town.

"Dad, who could possibly have done this? Do you have any clue?" I asked.

He pondered that a moment and replied, "Follow me to the house. I think I need a glass of bourbon."

His home in the Highland Park section of Saint Paul sits just a few blocks from the Mississippi River. It's a quiet area, and he lives in a house just a couple of years older than himself. He has offered several times to let me move in, but I have gently declined. That wouldn't be good for either of us, seeing as we both had romantic interests and needed our space.

But now Dad was alone again. After Mom died and he moved to the Twin Cities, he was in a funk for a long time before getting out and socializing. I was afraid Jane's death would knock him back into a depression.

After pouring himself some bourbon over ice, which I declined, we walked out to his back porch, where he maintains a thriving pepper colony. Amidst a profusion of red and green peppers of various sizes and intensity, we sat, and Dad let loose with a fountain of tears.

Seeing your parents cry is always unsettling. The last time I had witnessed it was at Mom's funeral. I let him go for a couple minutes until I couldn't take it any longer, then inquired about the police interrogating him.

"They wanted to know where I was in the last 24 hours," he said. "They determined Jane was...shot...sometime after midnight."

That confused me. Midnight? "But she was in her office..."

"She wasn't there when she was...murdered." He broke down again.

"Wait, I don't understand. So someone shot her, then took her to her office?"

He nodded and took a healthy swig. "She was just over here," he said, shaking his head. "I just saw her." He blubbered some more.

"When?"

"After work yesterday. She stopped by and brought me the newest Spenser novel." He tipped his glass toward the adjacent end table, where Robert B. Parker's *Potshot* sat.

"Dad, I know this is painful to talk about..."

"I've already told all this to the police," he responded. "I don't know anything. She seemed OK. Except for that weird thing."

"What weird thing?"

Dad stared into his glass for a moment. "She said she was thinking about taking a couple of days off to deal with something."

"What?"

"Didn't say. But she said, or maybe she didn't really say it but just hinted at it, that it was something she had to go out of town for. And no, she didn't say where."

"Did it sound like a family thing? What about her ex?"

"Bert? She never mentioned him. I don't know where he lives. I thought he was still in the Twin Cities, but I could be wrong."

"Her son?"

"Lex went east to start school. He's at Lehigh this year. Graduate program in management, I think. Charlie was in Miami, but she thought he headed west."

"Charlie?"

"Her older son."

"Oh, I don't know anything about him."

"She doesn't talk about him either." He caught himself. "Didn't. I got the feeling there was some tension there, like they were estranged."

"I hope you told the police that."

"I told them everything I knew, starting from when we first met to our trip to the Wisconsin Dells to how many times I spent the night at her place."

I didn't ask the question, but he saw the look on my face.

"Zero. I never spent the night there," he offered. He wasn't forthcoming, however, on how many times she spent the night at his place. And I really didn't need to know.

"Are you OK?"

"No, son, I'm not."

"You want me to stay here for a few days?"

He polished off his drink and got up to fix another. "I want you to go find out who could have done this. Why."

Johnny Scalabrino was expecting me to do just that. So far, in my few short years in the Scalabrino fold, I had come through. Somehow, this felt different, and I wasn't certain I could find the answers everyone expected of me.

8

Saturday, September 15

Freddie had one of those rare weekends off. The hammer blow of 9/11 had put the screaming brakes on the sports world. Games that weekend were postponed as officials scrambled to figure out what safety precautions needed to be implemented at stadiums across the nation.

Fans were left to mourn and contemplate the gravity of the situation without the distraction of sports.

This more than any event in my lifetime reaffirmed my belief that sporting contests are mere entertainment, diversions designed to pull humans out of their mundane, complicated, tragic lives for awhile and provide an outlet for all that pent-up aggression and stress.

Unfortunately, the amusement value of any event was always 50 percent. One wins, one loses. Rather than ease tensions, some teams exacerbated them. This seemed particularly true of teams in the Twin Cities, where sports were not always so fulfilling. A community of mostly losers was what we had.

So when Freddie offered to hang with me for the day, I took him up on it. With Emmie nowhere to be found, it seemed like the right thing to do, seeing as I didn't want to be alone with my thoughts.

For someone whose work routine had been stood on its head, Freddie seemed pretty relaxed. But I guess a rare weekend off in the fall will do that. The weather was great and the possibilities were endless, as long as we didn't want to attend a sporting event.

Naturally, Freddie wanted to hit a casino, lose ourselves in the clock-less environment of card tables, slot machines and roulette wheels. Given my history of weakened willpower in such a setting, I vetoed that notion. I was more amenable to touring a local brewery.

Everyone else had the same idea, unfortunately. With sports on hold, there were fewer entertainment options for local citizens. I learned later that theaters were jammed, casinos were bursting at the seams, and all the brew houses hosted long lines waiting to view and sample. After a glance at the line waiting outside the brewery we chose, I reconsidered.

I suggested we grab some beer, order a pizza and kick back listening to music at my place. For once, Freddie didn't fight me.

It wasn't as easy as it sounded. The liquor store on the corner looked like it had been looted. Gaping spaces in shelves attested to the reality of the dark days we were experiencing. There had been a run on booze, and the normal supply chain was interrupted by the week's events.

Although not my usual preference, the malt liquor appealed to me in the fact that it wasn't sold out. When we arrived at my place, the theme music I selected was the doomsday warbling of Jim Morrison on "The End." Seemed appropriate.

After one beer, Freddie was starving, so we dialed the number of Pie Hole and ordered a deep-dish sweep the kitchen number. Unfortunately, approximately four million other people in the metro area had the same idea, so it took an hour and a half to deliver the pizza.

In the meantime, we had polished off the hooch and I dispatched Freddie for more. He returned with reinforcements, including a pint of high-end bourbon, and we tackled the pizza.

"Did you find out who did it?" he asked between bites.

"No. The cops are still investigating. They think she was killed elsewhere."

"What, they kill her, then dump her body in the store?" he asked, dumbfounded. "Creepy."

"Probably to make it look like someone at La Scala did it."

"That's gotta be weird, seeing your boss croaked."

"Really weird," I said. "But she wasn't my boss anymore, remember?" We ate in silence awhile.

"So Emmie is still freaked about it, I guess."

"Can't find her. She won't answer my calls."

"Oh, man. You don't think something happened to her, do you, Beers?"

"No. Nothing like that. She's frightened. Or in shock, I guess." Of course, Freddie had planted the seed in my mind, so now I was worried something had happened to her. Why else wouldn't she answer my calls?

"I can look for her, if you want. Got nothing to do this weekend," he offered.

"Thanks, Freddie. If I knew where to look..."

"Maybe Gidget—"

"Called her. Nothing."

"Some other friend?"

"Yeah, like who?"

He drank in silence for a bit. "You should check her apartment. Maybe—"

"Been there, done that. No sign of her," I said. "She doesn't want to be found right now."

"Or...."

"Or nothing. Nothing happened to her. She's fine.

"So I guess you just sit and wait."

Freddie hit the nail on the head. I was helpless to do anything to find either Emmie or the killer. Or was I?

"Freddie, I think we need some company. Female company."

His grim expression quickly changed to a grin. "Now you're talking!"

Unfortunately for him, it wasn't the kind of female company he had in mind.

9

"Why dintja tell me da goof was gonna be heah?" Lena seemed a bit put out when she saw Freddie lounging on the couch, sucking down another cocktail.

As with many things in life, I was clueless about their relationship. Freddie and Lena had hooked up for a brief fling in the recent past but seemed cordial since. Now something had flared up between them, or Lena had just realized how exasperating Freddie could be on an ongoing basis.

"Sorry, Lena. Do you have any info for me?"

"Got any wine?"

I got her a glass of merlot and she pulled some papers out of her purse. Wisely, Freddie remained silent while she showed me the results of her research.

"Tina comin' ovah?" she asked.

"No, she had something going on," I said. "She thought she would have some news tomorrow."

Lena's printout had a list of names, addresses and phone numbers. At the top of the list were Mr. and Mrs. Roy Slayton, with an address in Shelbyville, Indiana. I called and got a woman I assumed was Emmie's mother. After an awkward introduction, I explained that Emmie wasn't answering my calls, and I wanted to know whether she had heard from her daughter. No, she hadn't, but would contact me if she did.

After hanging up, I had a weird sensation. The conversation had been odd, seeing as her mother did not seem very alarmed that her daughter was MIA. Perhaps they were estranged, I thought, or Emmie had a history of being incommunicado.

The other numbers on the list were her younger brother and older sister, neither of whom was available. I left messages asking for a callback if they heard from Emmie.

"Shouldn't you be checking on the deceased's relatives?" Freddie asked.

"No, that's a job for the police," I responded. "This is one case I'm trying not to get real involved in."

"I thought you already were."

"Just to find Emmie. And I need to do that anyway, since I have a vested interest."

"She takin' it pretty hawd," Lena offered.

"To say the least. This is the longest we've been out of touch since we met."

"Lemme know if ya heah from da family," Lena said on her way out.

"Not sticking around?" Freddie asked. "We've got pizza."

She gave him a withering stare before departing.

"What's that all about?" I asked.

"Don't know. She's been rather icy the last couple of times we bumped into each other."

"Knowing Lena, it was something you did, Freddie. Or said."

"Probably right. But I can't keep track of everything I say or do."

When the pizza was gone and the alcohol stash once again depleted, Freddie wanted to hit The Crater, our frequent haunt in downtown Minneapolis. I wasn't in the mood. I just wanted to put on some more music, curl up and wait for the miasma to pass— and Emmie to return to me. Freddie didn't want to sit around watching me sulk. He said he was flying to Cincinnati in the morning to visit his brother. For now, he was heading over to the U to mingle with the coeds. I was certain if Lena were still around, she would give him another icy stare.

AS EVENING WORE ON, I was no closer to getting any answers. Not that I had made that great of an effort, but the usual fall-in-my-lap solution hadn't happened. I was getting ready to put my music away and call it a night when Tina phoned.

"Good thing I have a lingering talent for law enforcement," she said. For a brief time, Tina had given up her cosmetics post to pursue a long-held dream of becoming a detective. She was quickly disillusioned by the reality of mundane school patrols and other crap assignments.

"You found Emmie?" I asked eagerly.

"Not as such. But we did find out where she last used her credit card."

"We?"

"Anthony and me. Detective Cuccia. She used it at a filling station on the outskirts of Chicago."

"So she's in Chicago somewhere."

"Not necessarily. She could have been passing through. This was yesterday about 9 p.m. Probably heading east."

As I ruminated on that, Tina continued.

"There's more. Jane made some calls to a 310 number."

"What's that?"

"Area code for Los Angeles. Did she know someone there?"

"I have no idea."

"Maybe a relative or secret admirer? Or someone who wanted her dead?"

"How the heck should I know? Whose number is it?"

"Traced to a Mexican restaurant in Torrance. Cuccia is contacting them now to try to find out more."

"How do you know Cuccia?" I asked. By my reckoning, he was on the Scalabrino payroll, the inside connection to the police department. But Tina had never mentioned him before.

"Oh, we go way back," she replied. "Way back."

I wasn't sure I wanted to know more.

"I put in a call to her son Lex but haven't heard back yet."

"There's a detective following the family angle," Tina said. "Not sure what they've found out, but I guess they know about the sons. And the ex."

"Yeah, where is he?"

"Dunno. Another detective is looking for him."

"How many detectives do they have on this case?"

"Oh, man, it's a shitload. For some reason, they're pouring all resources into this. I guess because it's so close to...y'know."

The specter of Sept. 11 loomed over everything and would for some time to come, I assumed.

10

Sunday, September 16

I didn't think things could get worse, but of course they did.

It started early when Dad called to say there were police cars outside his house with lights flashing. He hung up after telling me they were coming up the walk to the front door.

I threw clothes on and headed down to the parking ramp to get my car. If Dad was being interrogated, I wanted to be around for support.

Unfortunately, by the time I got to his house in Highland Park, the police cars and Dad were gone. A neighbor saw me at the front door and came over to report that he had been taken away in cuffs.

Oh shit.

On the way to the police station, Freddie called. He wanted me to come to the airport to help him out.

"Can't right now, Fred. Heading down to the police station. Dad has been brought in for questioning, apparently."

"Oh." There was a heavy note of disappointment in his voice.

"What's the matter? You miss your flight?"

"Well...in a way."

"Freddie, I don't have time to pick you up right now. Maybe you can catch a later flight."

"They may not let me," he replied.

"Freddie, what's going on?"

"I'm being detained. They let me make one call. I thought you could come vouch for me."

It wasn't registering, but he continued.

"They sorta took me to this holding room. I got to make one call, so I called you. If you can't help me, maybe you can get Lena to come?"

"What the hell did you do this time?" I yelled.

"Look, it's not my fault." Every time Freddie got into trouble, this was the first excuse out of his mouth. I should have expected it.

"It's just a misunderstanding is all. I was checking my luggage and I told the airline guy to be careful with it because I just bought it."

"Yeah, and...?"

"I told him I didn't want it to go off somewhere."

"Yeah, so?"

"Go off? He thought I meant a bomb. I was just saying I didn't want it to get lost, y'know? Like they always do. They're so careless with luggage."

"So you got detained for that?"

"Obviously, everyone is skittish right now. They arrest people if they look funny."

"Freddie, I can't help you. I have to go see about my dad."

"That's OK. Hopefully, they'll check my bag and see it's just got clothes and shit in it. Then I can go."

The police station was sparsely populated on a Sunday morning. Everyone at church, I thought, or perhaps too hung over from Saturday night to cause a ruckus.

The front desk sergeant offered no information on Dad and told me to wait on the bench across from the counter. So I waited. About 20 minutes after I arrived, Detective Farraday walked out of a back room and conferred briefly with the sergeant. He looked up, saw me and nodded his head imperceptibly. Then he returned to the back room.

When my phone rang, I assumed it was Freddie being a pest again.

"What now, Freddie? I'm still busy."

"Hey, son. It's Dad."

"Oh...I thought you were Freddie."

"They took me for questioning down to the station."

"I know. I'm here."

"You're here?"

"In the waiting area."

"Well...you might as well go home. Looks like I'm going to be here for awhile."

"What's going on?"

"They want to know about Jane."

"I guessed that."

"They want to know *everything* about Jane. From the time I met her till today. Or I guess the last time we were together."

"I thought you already told them everything."

"They want to hear it again. In case I forgot something."

"Are you a suspect?"

"No, no, no...well..."

His unspoken thought was the same one I had. Why were they grilling him again unless they suspected he had something to do with her murder? The spouse is always the chief suspect in a murder case, and if the spouse isn't around, the boyfriend will do, I figured.

"Hang in there, Dad. And call me if you need anything."

"Will do, son."

There was nothing I could do here except kill time, so I called Freddie back.

"You still need a pickup?"

"Yeah. Doesn't look like I'm going to Cincy today."

"You're not under arrest or anything, are you?"

"No. They found out I had nothing but jockeys and T-shirts and jeans in the bag. Of course, that was after they destroyed it."

"Destroyed it?"

"Yeah. Took it off somewhere and blew it up. I'm telling you, Beers, this terror alert stuff is getting crazy."

"I'll be there in 20. Be waiting at the Northwest pickup."

11

Monday, September 17

No more incidents marred an otherwise quiet Sunday. I retrieved Dad from the police station in the afternoon after he had convinced the authorities that he knew nothing about Jane's demise. Still, they advised him to stick around in case they wanted to quiz him some more.

As the workweek began, the store continued to have an eerie vibe. Business was down as customers eschewed the simple pleasure of retail purchasing. Perhaps they were fearful of going out among strangers, any one of whom could be a secret terrorist, waiting to blow up unsuspecting innocent bystanders. The national psyche was fucked up and wasn't going to get better any time soon.

Perhaps they just didn't want to fight the traffic. The street construction project had created major barriers to the efficient flow of commerce.

All thoughts of securing the store had been put on hold, however, in light of the most recent tragedy. When Salmon Foster arrived in my office and shut the door, I expected he wanted to resurrect that line of endeavor. What followed left me stunned.

"Sit down, Biersovich," he announced.

"I am sitting, sir."

"Oh...yes, I see." He was pacing, exhibiting an unease I had never seen previously. "We have a bit of a situation here...I'm not going to sugarcoat it."

"I know it's bad, Mr. Foster. First 9/11, then Jane..."

"About that." He stopped pacing and stared at some unseen image on the blank side wall of my humble office. "Something will happen today and I want you to get ready." He paused long enough for my mental jukebox to kick into gear on that last phrase. The Temptations warbled "Get Ready" in my head until he spoke again.

"Something is going to happen and you need to know about it in case the police ask you. Before Jane...died..."

He couldn't bring himself to say she was murdered, which she was. Why? Could he be responsible? Was I in danger from Foster? Was he spilling his guts before offing me? A cold fear crept across my skin.

"Before that, we had a little misunderstanding. She was fighting me on something."

"What, sir?"

He started pacing again. "Jane was not happy here. I could tell. I was trying to help her out, you see."

He was being obtuse and the day was wearing on. I just wanted him to spit it out and be done with it. And not with a bullet at the end, I hoped.

"Could you get to the point, Mr. Foster? I have to work on—"

"You're involved because it was you I was trying to move into her office," he blurted.

"Huh? I don't get it. She already has an assistant...had," I replied.

"Not as her assistant. No. As a replacement."

Now his words made even less sense than before. Replacement? What did that mean? Jane was quitting? Had she given notice? Did she find another job elsewhere, a better paying job? Surely she wouldn't be killed for finding another employer. The questions raced through my brain, then Foster spoke again.

"The board decided Jane would be better in some other capacity. I selected you as her replacement."

"What? You're kidding, right?"

Despite Foster's uncanny resemblance to the great comic actor Leslie Nielsen, he was not being funny. It was no joke. I was too flabbergasted to speak. Fortunately, Foster continued with his explanation.

It seems Jane had made some decisions that pissed off a certain board member. This person suggested to the full board that someone else might perform better in the position.

I could guess who that unnamed board member was. He was pacing in front of me.

Foster had begun eviction proceedings, and Jane was resisting. He had sent her a memo instructing her to move out of her office by the 10th of September, and she had refused. He was now in the precarious position of explaining this delicate situation, which the police obviously had learned about when combing through Jane's office.

"They're coming for me this morning, Biersovich. You might want to inform Mr. Scalabrino in case he wants to send someone...to watch over things."

Foster knew I had a closer relationship to the big boss than he did, and I was also chummy with Scalabrino's cousin, Joe T. We had worked together on a number of cases, and I was a not-infrequent visitor at the Scalabrino mansion off the parkway. While Foster had the power, I had the access.

Foster left before I gathered my wits sufficiently to inform him that no way in hell would I replace Jane. I didn't want to advance my career—I wanted to leave it. Just like in the Billy Joel tune: *If that's movin' up then I'm movin' out.*

If I thought the complications of my employment at La Scala were difficult before, they had become exponentially more convoluted now. I was personally embroiled in a situation over which I had no control and no previous knowledge.

Maybe Emmie was right to run away. And I should follow.

12

The more I thought about Foster's revelation, the less sense it made. What decisions had Jane made that could possibly have bent Foster so out of shape as to want to fire her?

She was the vice president in charge of facilities, which meant she dealt with all aspects of the physical structure, from renovations to parking to painting contractors. I, by extension, had been her subordinate, dealing with the security aspects of the structure—doors, locks, alarms, shoplifters and so on.

Then Scalabrino had broken off my duties into a separate function, so Jane and I essentially worked as peers, although she still had her title and much larger salary. I remained a peon in the scheme of things.

But apparently Foster wanted me to replace her. As a vice president? That couldn't be right. I had made known several times in my two and a half years at La Scala that I didn't want to make a career out of it. In fact, I had tendered my resignation more than once, only to be sucked back in by the inevitable raise and increase in responsibility.

Not to mention proximity to my main squeeze.

Emmie's absence was disturbing. She had been off the grid for three days and no word. It was uncharacteristic of her. She could at least call to say she was OK.

It wasn't long before the other shoe dropped again.

"YOU DIDN'T FIND the secretary—we did." Farraday had strolled into my office while I was playing solitaire, one of the few computer functions I had mastered. A pair of detectives flanked him, and there were two uniformed officers outside the door.

"You need to come clean about what else you're hiding," he said.

"I have no idea what you're talking about," I said.

"Emerald Slayton. Picked her up at her parents' house in Indiana. We'll get to the bottom of this, Biersovich." He gave me a stern look before exiting with his posse.

Emmie was at her parents' house? Had she been there when I called, and they were hiding the fact? I still couldn't figure out why she wouldn't get in touch with me. And now she was in police custody. I couldn't imagine that she had any useful information to impart. And no way could I envision that she had anything to do with Jane's murder.

On the plus side, at least she was alive and safe, and I could dismiss the worry of peril raised by Freddie.

A commotion in the hall roused me, and I stepped out to see Salmon Foster surrounded by Farraday and crew. As I approached, I heard Farraday telling Foster: "...and we can do this the easy way or the hard way. Easy way, you cooperate fully. Hard way, we bring out the cuffs. Your choice."

"What's going on here?" I said, causing everyone to turn in my direction.

"Stay out of this," one of the other detectives said.

"Mr. Scalabrino needs to know—"

"Sir, I need you to step back out of the way."

"It's OK, Biersovich," Foster said. "I just need to clear up a few things. You understand." He flashed me a smile, a rarity I couldn't recall seeing in a very long time. I could tell it was forced and unnatural for him.

"I'll alert Mr. Scalabrino," I said, as they escorted him into the elevator.

Before calling the boss, I put in a call to Cuccia to find out what he knew about Emmie. All he could tell me was that she was brought to a police station in Indianapolis and was being interrogated. He would try to find out more later.

Joe T wasn't surprised when I informed him of the latest developments. The big boss wasn't around, however, because he left for New York City to check on relatives missing in the wake of the Twin Towers disaster. Communication with Ground Zero was impossible.

"What should I do?" I asked. I could have predicted his response.

"Sit tight," he said. "I'll be there later."

Tina and Lena responded to my calls and were in my office in a few minutes.

"Yeah, my guy heard she had been picked up," Tina said. "Cops don't like it much when a witness to murder goes on the lam."

"She didn't witness anything," I replied. "She walked in and discovered Jane after the fact."

"Still."

"Ya tawk ta her yet?" Lena asked.

"No, she never answered my calls."

"Maybe she wised up an' dropped ya ass," Lena said with a smirk. Her attempt at levity missed the mark and only pissed me off further.

"I'm serious here," I said sternly, "and I hope you'll take this seriously also." Lena was duly admonished.

"Who's running the show?" Tina asked.

"Joe T is. At least I think he is. Foster will have lots of questions to answer and could be gone for awhile."

"You going to Indiana?" Tina asked.

I hadn't seriously considered it with everything else going on, but when Tina voiced the concept, it seemed imperative.

"I want to, but I don't see how I can leave now."

"We can covah ya," Lena said. "Wit' Jane dead an' Fostah out, who ya gonna ansah to?"

Joe T, of course. I would have to clear it with him, and that would be tricky with the current short-handed staff. But he had to understand my worry that Emmie hadn't left willy-nilly. She was terrified of something. I had to find out what.

13

Naturally, Joe T dismissed my plea outright when I called him back. Too much going on for me to take off at the moment. If Foster returned and things settled down, he would reconsider.

Meanwhile, he wanted me to get the security enhancements rolling. Also, I was to speak with the rest of the managers and find out whether they had any notions about Jane's murder.

"Look in her personnel file and see if there's anything. Talk to the veeps on site. She was over maintenance, right? Didn't we have a problem with them before? Talk to what's his name..."

"Don Anderson."

"Anderson. See what he knows. Someone got in here with her body, outside store hours. Check the cleaning crew also."

"So you think it's an inside job."

"No, just covering the bases," Joe T said. "Sometimes people say things they don't tell the cops. Rumors. You take good notes. We might find something someone says that the cops didn't get."

"Can I get Lena and Tina to help me?"

"Yeah, whatever you need." He planned to be in the executive suite in the afternoon, so I had work to do before he arrived.

The girls were more than willing to pitch in. Lena agreed to tackle the personnel files in the computer system. She thought she could bypass red tape and get her buddies in the IT department, Dweep and Kweep, to give her access. Tina said she would meet with Anderson and the maintenance crew. That left me to grill the suits.

Actually, pantsuits. Other than Foster, the upper management of La Scala Minneapolis was all-female. Perhaps his move to replace Jane with me was an attempt to get more testosterone into the store's decision-making processes.

I was speaking with the head of merchandise when we were interrupted by a commotion in the executive suite. One of the detectives I recognized from earlier was there, along with a cop in uniform.

"Mr. Biersovich, please come with us." The detective was motioning me to follow.

"No can do. I've got orders from the owner to—"

"Cuff him, Stocker." The policeman wasted no time in whipping out a pair of handcuffs and securing me before I could commit some criminal act. There were gasps of horror from the small crowd of managers and secretaries that had emerged from offices to witness the scene.

"What's the deal?" I protested. "With Mr. Foster out—"

"We're going to the station," the detective said. "Bring him."

The officer grabbed my arm and pulled me toward the elevators.

"Can I make a call?" I yelped.

"Later," the detective replied. We rode down and they dragged me across the street, around the construction pit, to a waiting black-and-white at the curb. The stares of a thousand pairs of eyes stabbed my back, wondering what flavor of desperado had been in their midst in downtown on a pleasant September day. Perhaps a killer?

THE INTERROGATION ROOM was similar to the ones you see on crime shows, except much smaller. Basically, just a desk and two chairs, plus a motivational poster on one wall featuring a shadowed outline of a man behind bars: *Truth—It may not set you free, but there's no substitute.*

Thankfully, I was uncuffed. I was left to ruminate on my fate for nearly an hour before the door opened and Farraday walked in. He offered coffee, which I declined, then sat across from me while sipping from a paper cup.

After two minutes of silence, I couldn't take it anymore. "You going to tell me why I'm here?" I asked.

"You seem to have a bit of a problem," he responded coolly. "And the quicker you come clean, the faster we can get this thing solved."

"I don't know what 'problem' you're talking about," I replied.

"Don't you, though?"

Whatever game he was playing, I refused to go along. I sat quietly, waiting for him to lay out his cards, humming inside my head the tune to Simon & Garfunkel's "The Sound of Silence." The tactic worked, because he broke first.

"You want to tell me about your career advancement plan?" He asked it with a sneer.

"Again, I don't know what you're talking about."

"Don't be funny. We know all about you moving into the victim's office."

Foster's office putsch came back to me. "I had nothing to do with that."

Farraday smirked.

"Mr. Foster just told me about that. It's all his doing. I'm not looking to move up at La Scala. I'm content where I am."

"Not the way I heard it," he retorted.

What was he referring to—something Foster had told him? Was Foster trying to pin the murder on me? Was that his way of keeping the heat off himself and resolving the situation so the store could get back to normal? The only reason he would do that would be...if Foster were the killer.

"I don't know what Foster told you, but I don't know anything about why Jane Mertin was killed. Nothing. Do I need to speak with an attorney?" I asked.

"No, no need for that. You're not being charged with anything. Yet."

"Then I want to leave," I demanded.

"First I need to hear everything you know about the deceased."

I told him what little I knew. That I had become acquainted with Jane while working at the paper. That she was captain of her over-40 soccer team that I wrote a feature about, leading to her offering me a job at La Scala. That I was her assistant for a time but really didn't intersect with her much on a daily basis. That she and my father had developed a relationship. That my girlfriend served as her secretary. And that was about all I could tell him.

Farraday finished off his coffee and left the room without saying a word. Another half-hour of waiting wasn't doing my bladder any favors. When I couldn't take it anymore, I peeked out the door. The hallway was vacant, so I went searching for the men's room. I found it down an interconnecting corridor and soon felt better.

Exiting the men's room, I spotted Farraday walking toward me.

"What are you doing?!" he demanded.

"Peeing," I said. "Is that OK?"

"You need to ask before you go wandering off."

"Well, you weren't around, and I had to go. So are you done with me? Can I leave now?"

"You haven't told me anything useful yet."

My blood was boiling, and I should have kept my cool, but I had reached the breaking point. "Look, I've told you everything I know, which is nothing. I had nothing to do with the murder, my dad had nothing to do with it, and Emmie Slayton had nothing to do with it. Maybe you should go look for someone who knows something!"

Normally, that type of antagonism does little to advance your cause. In this instance, it seemed to work. Farraday regarded me with a calculating gaze, then said I could leave. No warnings to stay in town and alert him to any new information I gathered or old recollections that magically popped into my head. Just a cold, steely glare that I could feel on my back as I exited.

They say there are a handful of major turning points in one's lifetime. I felt I was on the verge of such a moment. The future was a big question mark. A paralyzing fear gripped me, along with a certainty that I was heading to a bad outcome.

14

O
n the drive back to the store, I determined that the only
way I'd get my dad, Emmie and myself in the clear was to
find the culprit. If the cops didn't do it, I would have to,
because we'd never be exonerated otherwise.

My initial thought was that Foster had dumped suspicion on me
to divert it from himself. It was like a tennis rally and I wanted to
make sure the ball landed back in his court. I would need Lena and
Tina for that.

When I got back to my desk, there was a memo on it from the
finance office authorizing me to proceed with the security camera
installation. About time! If only that had come a week or two
earlier, we might not be facing this dilemma.

Tina strolled in shortly after I hung up with Lights, Camera,
Action, the company that was recommended for the installation.
She closed the door and sat at Lena's desk.

"The cops are going to release the body to the family on
Wednesday," she said. "I think they're lining up the funeral for
Saturday. And I talked with Anderson. He's up to his neck with
pest control."

"Pest control?"

"Yeah. The street construction seems to have stirred up the
critters. We've got rats running around the basement and ants in
the break room."

Tina's report triggered an old Masters of Reality tune in my
head: *Ants in the kitchen, thought I'd let you know...*

"They're pretty localized right now but If we start seeing them
in the retail areas, it won't be good," she added.

"Good Lord."

"So I don't think he had anything to do with the murder. He said he got along fine with Jane and had just gotten a raise. We can check that with payroll."

"Any of his crew?"

"The only one on staff full time right now is Bradley. He's such a goof, it's hard to imagine him being capable of killing a fly."

"True that."

"He would probably shoot himself if he handled a gun. And they haven't hired the fall interns yet. Anderson's taking his time to find someone on the ball."

"So, the opposite of Bradley."

"Exactly."

In a bit of odd occurrence that couldn't have been scripted, Bradley walked into my office at that moment.

"Dude, this the furniture you moving?" he asked. He waved a piece of paper at my desk and looked around. I was at a loss to respond to this non sequitur. Tina gaped at him like she had just been caught smoking in the girls' room.

Bradley looked at the paper he was holding, then read from it: "Relocate desk, chairs, cabinets...blah blah blah...office nine two two...etcetera...executive suite D...blah blah...on or before September 14th...yadda yadda yadda...signed, Mister Eff."

So there was a paper trail on this office coup. Foster had directed maintenance to move my gear into Jane's suite. It was supposed to happen last week.

"There must be some mistake," I said.

Bradley looked at the paper again, then looked back at me. "No, I just checked." He held the paper out to me. I didn't take it but Tina snatched it from him.

After scanning it, she said, "What the fuck, Beers?"

"Yeah, dude, what the eff?" Bradley echoed.

"I was going to tell you about this—"

"I'm sure," Tina retorted.

"Look, I just found out about this from Foster. I had nothing to do with it. In fact, this may have something to do with Jane's...what happened to her."

Tina made me tell exactly what Foster had said. Fortunately, my notepad provided all the pertinent details. When I was done, Tina just shook her head and left.

"So we gonna do this?" Bradley asked.

"Do what?" I replied.

"Move your shit. Like, down the hall. I don't have all day."

"No, we're not moving my office. I'm staying put."

"But Mister Eff said—"

"I don't give an eff what Mister Eff said. I'm staying in this office. Besides, Suite D is a crime scene, so we can't disturb it anyway."

Bradley mustered up his single brain cell and thought about that for a second. "Yeah, that sounds legit. Well, call me if you change your mind." And he was off.

DETECTIVE CUCCIA phoned after lunch to report on Emmie's interrogation in Indianapolis. The only thing he could tell me was that she was released to the custody of her parents. He surmised that she was not a suspect "at this time."

I wanted to ask why she didn't call me, but Cuccia wouldn't know the answer. Call her again? Perhaps the grilling had shaken her out of whatever malaise she was suffering, and she would tell me what was going on with her. As I feared, the call went to voicemail once again. I was despairing of ever speaking with her.

The only thing to do, I figured, was go AWOL myself, drive to Indiana and see her face to face. She might be paranoid about speaking over the phone. Did she think she was next in line to be killed? Did the murderer want both of them out of the way?

Try as I might, I couldn't envision a scenario where Emmie was involved in anything with Jane that would make her a target. She was a secretary, for God's sake. To the facilities director, no less. Could there be anything less controversial?

Just as I was making final plans to go off the reservation, I got three calls that changed things. First, Freddie rang to say I would have to go out with him Tuesday night to celebrate his birthday, since his trip to see his brother had been thwarted. Then the security company called and said a rep would be out shortly to do a walk-through. The kicker was when Joe T phoned. He said he would come in to observe the camera plan.

Freddie, I could blow off. Security guy—he could be postponed. Joe T, however, didn't take no for an answer.

15

The account executive for Lights, Camera, Action was named Peter Templeton. He arrived in my office with an assistant he called Turk.

Templeton said his plan was to provide 48 cameras for the 10 floors of the building (including the basement). I could situate them wherever I wanted but he had recommendations. For starters, inside the elevators, at the loading ramp, on the front doors and in the first-floor stairwell. Cameras on each level could be positioned to cover most of the floor if they were put in each corner.

That sounded reasonable to me, and I was ready to sign off on it, but he insisted on a walk-through, with Turk marking the locations on a clipboard.

Starting at the ninth floor, we worked our way down. I generally agreed to everything he suggested. When we got to the basement, he had Turk total up the locations. They came to 52. Apparently, he was getting paid by the camera and had inflated the cost by 10 percent.

"But don't worry—you'll save on property and liability insurance by installing these, so the cost will be offset," he argued. "Just sign here, initial here...and here. We'll get started on Thursday."

I thought about running it by Salmon Foster but figured he was up to his neck in problems. Besides, I had been given the green light, so I signed. After all, I had been advocating this very thing almost from the day I had arrived at La Scala.

Joe T never showed up for the tour, which was unusual for him. He was normally good for his word. But I didn't give it a second thought. He probably had some last-minute job assigned by the boss.

With the install a couple of days off, I again pondered a road trip to Indiana. I could get there late Monday night, have all day Tuesday to talk with Emmie and find out what was going on, then return home Wednesday. Yeah, that would work. No one would miss me for a couple of days. Just had to get the blessing of Joe T—that was a tricky feat.

I spent the rest of my shift working up the courage to tell Joe T what I wanted to do. I had even convinced myself that he would encourage me to go when I explained how Emmie might be an integral part of the investigation. She might open up to me more than she did to the cops, although I was certain she knew nothing.

In the end, I decided to call Joe T from the road. Not give him a chance to say no. Tell him there was an urgent situation I had to look into that required my presence, since Emmie wouldn't communicate with me by phone. Yeah, try the old "it's better to beg for forgiveness than ask permission" routine.

On the way home, I dialed Freddie to deliver the bad news: Can't hang with you on your birthday, chum. Have to take a rain check.

Freddie was disappointed, naturally, but when he heard what I was planning, he wanted in on the trip. After considering for a few moments, I decided that having someone else to split the driving was a positive, even if it was Freddie. I told him I'd take him along if he could get ready in 30 minutes.

BY 6 P.M. we were on the road. I calculated we would arrive in Indianapolis after midnight. Freddie convinced me that getting a motel room would be preferable to camping out in Emmie's parents' front yard.

After we passed Madison, Wisconsin, Freddie took over the driving. I bit the bullet and called Joe T. Surprisingly, he wasn't upset about my trek across state lines. I could tell he was preoccupied with something, perhaps the thing that kept him away from the store that afternoon. I assured him I would be back on Wednesday in case he needed me.

When we made a pit stop, I got a call from Tina.

"Where the hell are you, Beers?"

"Hello to you too, Tina."

"I know you're not at your apartment and you're not at The Crater. Are you by chance going to see Emmie?"

Uncanny. But not unprecedented. Tina's deductive skills were once again on target.

"I'm taking a road trip, yes."

"She may not see you."

"I'll take that chance," I replied. "Besides, we're sort of involved with each other, so I have a vested interest in getting her to return."

"You want me to call the detective and see—"

"No! Don't call him. I need this to be between Emmie and me."

"And Freddie," she replied, with what I surmised was a grin, if that can be relayed over a phone line.

"How did you...never mind. I'll talk to you later." I hung up before she could give me the requisite Freddie warning. Didn't need it. I was on high alert for Freddie-like situations. So far, so good.

"Tina tracked you down?" Freddie asked. "Man, that woman is something!"

"Yeah. She's got some kind of radar."

"I might have to offer her a bit of the old Freddie charm."

"What? No. No, no, no. Stay away from Tina," I said. "We've got enough trouble at the store already."

"Beers, that stings."

"I'm just saying to keep your mitts off if you know what's good for you. Tina isn't someone to mess around with. She was a cop for awhile, y'know."

"I can handle myself," Freddie replied.

"No, you can't. Not with Tina. Trust me. Keep fishing in the kiddie pool at the U. If you get crossways with Tina, you may not survive. And I'm not kidding."

Freddie was quiet after that, probably considering the risk factor and how he could mitigate it. Knowing him like I did, my warning had probably only heightened his resolve to add a Tina notch to his conquest belt. Perhaps I shouldn't worry about it. I knew Tina could handle herself. Maybe Freddie needed to learn the hard way.

I thought about warning Tina, but she certainly didn't need it. She was savvier than a pack of Girl Scouts. She could withstand a

Freddie advance without straining. Whether Freddie would survive wasn't my concern.

16

Tuesday, September 18

Y ou mean she doesn't even know you're coming?" Freddie put his forkful of scrambled eggs down and stared at me with incredulity across the breakfast table at the roadside motel we had found outside Indianapolis.

"I didn't want to give her the opportunity to bolt."

"Beers, I think you may have screwed the pooch. She obviously doesn't want to talk to you. You think sneaking up on her is a good idea?"

"It's not sneaking up," I said indignantly. "I'm here to help her get through whatever fears she has about returning to the store. She's obviously in shock."

"Yeah, and this won't shock her, I'm sure," Freddie replied sarcastically.

He had a point, but I wasn't going to concede it. I needed to see Emmie in person, talk with her and find out what was in her head. It had been four days since I had last seen her, which seemed like a lifetime. Excluding my London trip, it was the longest we had been apart since we started dating almost a year ago.

Emmie's parents lived in a town called Shelbyville, about a half-hour southeast of Indianapolis. Freddie didn't know it, but I was planning to see her alone. He would have to cool his jets while I completed my mission.

Unfortunately, I knew Freddie all too well and was certain he would resist me on this. So I formulated a subterfuge.

"Dude, I've got to run down to that pharmacy we passed down the road. Why don't you get packed up and check out while I'm gone?"

"What do you need? Maybe I have some," he said.

I had a feeling he would ask that. "Some antifungal cream."

"Hey, I have some of that. The one with all the bugs on the commercial."

Damnit. "No, that doesn't work for me. I need the other one. I'll see you in a bit."

Before Freddie could respond, I lammed and hit the highway. Using a map I had found in the motel office, I made my way down the interstate toward Shelbyville. With only a minimum of backtracking and stopping for directions twice, I found myself at the curb in front of the Slayton residence. It was a modest two-story home in a cul-de-sac behind an elementary school. Just before I exited the car, Freddie called, but I let it go to voicemail.

It was nearing 10 a.m., so everyone should be up. Confidently, I strode to the front door and rang the bell. When it opened, I came face to face with a woman who I assumed was Emmie's mother. She had similar facial features, some wrinkles around the eyes that added character, and deep blue irises, unlike Emmie's green. She was wearing a gray button-up sweater over a white long-sleeve shirt and tan pants. She was sporting a pleasant smile and looked like she was ready for a day at the country club.

"Mrs. Slayton?" I said.

"Yes?"

"I'm Jim Biersovich. Emmie and I work together at La Scala."

"Oh." Her smile quickly faded.

"We're also...dating," I added. "I came out here because I'm worried about Emmie."

"No need to be," she said dismissively, looking like she was ready to close the door in my face.

"If I could just speak with her for a minute."

"I'm afraid that's not going to happen." Then she did close the door.

What the Sam Hill was going on? Was the family holding Emmie against her will? Or was she harboring some resentment against me? I had no clue but was determined to get to the bottom of it. I had come too far to turn around now. I rang the bell again persistently until the door reopened. This time there was a young guy who greeted me.

"Look, bro, you need to step off. Emmie doesn't want to see you. So just go away." The guy was wearing a blue polo shirt and jeans and looked to be around Emmie's age, maybe a couple years younger. Obviously, her brother.

"I need to hear her say it," I responded. "I'm not leaving until I see her."

"Suit yourself," he said, slamming the door.

I stepped back a bit to look at the upstairs windows to see whether Emmie was watching. Curtains were closed, but she could be peeking through the cracks. Or perhaps she was sedated and didn't have any idea her family was keeping us apart.

My cell rang again, but it wasn't Freddie.

"Beers, where y'at?" Lena asked.

"Running an errand," I replied. "What's going on?"

"Ya might wanna get down heah pronto. Rat just bit a customah."

"What?!"

"Dey runnin' wild up in heah," she explained. "Got da pest control goin' round but dey jus' movin' 'em from one place ta da othah. Dere's a lawyah up wit' Fostah right now threatenin' ta sue."

Holy crap. Always something. But even if I left immediately, I wouldn't get to the store before closing.

"Do what you can. Get Anderson and his crew to help out. I'm out of pocket until tomorrow. If you get in a real bind, call Joe T."

"Whatevah you doin', I hope it's more fun dan dis." She hung up before I could tell her it wasn't.

I had come a long way to sort this out and wasn't ready to give up just yet. So I started ringing the bell and banging on the door. When the door flew open, it was the brother again. He pushed me back off the front step and yelled, "I'm gonna kick your ass!"

As he advanced on me, I slowly backed toward the sidewalk, getting into a wrestling crouch. I didn't remember many moves from my high school gym class, but I thought I might at least get him to the ground, where it would be tougher to pummel me.

Then I remembered that he supposedly was under house arrest. Was he wearing an ankle bracelet? Was it for beating up someone?

He was almost upon me when a voice from the porch said "Stop!" It was Emmie. The brother turned to look. "Go back inside, Hermie." He stared at me for a few seconds more before retreating.

Heading up to the door, I saw this as a sign that Emmie was ready to end her self-imposed exile and come back with me. Wrong. She held her hands up as I approached.

"I'm not going back, Jim," she said.

"But why, Emmie?"

She just shook her head.

"You belong in the Twin Cities—with me," I argued. Her eyes began to water, and I sensed a full-on blubber about to erupt.

"Just tell me what the problem is, and I'll help you fix it." She sniffled, and a few tears ran down her cheeks. "I need you," I pleaded.

She shook her head again and walked back inside, where she slowly closed the door.

It was a bewildering kiss-off, without the kiss.

Either I could bang on the door all day in a futile attempt to change Emmie's mind, or I could admit defeat for now and head back. I chose the latter.

When I dialed Freddie's number, he didn't answer, so I left a message. Driving back to the motel, I dissected the nuances of my encounter with Emmie but failed to come up with any reasonable conclusion. It was simply baffling. There was no conceivable connection I could make between Emmie and Jane's murder. Perhaps in time she would come around, I concluded.

Arriving at the motel, I saw no sign of Freddie. The office provided no help. He had checked out, and they never saw him after that. I rang Freddie again but still no response. The day was wearing on, and I needed to get back to the Twin Cities to deal with the ongoing predicament there. I decided to give Freddie another half-hour to call me back before hitting the road.

By the time I got back on the interstate, I had convinced myself that Freddie got pissed at me for ditching him and somehow found a ride back home. He would be mad for awhile, but eventually he would see my side of things. Besides, if I couldn't change Emmie's mind, his presence wouldn't have done a thing.

It was almost midnight when I crawled into bed, slowed by nighttime construction along the route and a general weariness that prompted me to stop frequently for coffee. Of course, all that caffeine took its toll, and I wound up staring at the ceiling for quite a while before drifting off.

17

Wednesday, September 19

The demands for my attention started well before I arrived at La Scala. While drinking coffee in my kitchen, I got two calls, one from Tina and one from Salmon Foster.

Tina chewed my ear off with complaints about the infestation of insects and rodents. She had found critters crawling through a mascara box and was demanding a full frontal assault until the problem was solved. I told her I had the exterminator on the top of my list for the day.

Foster ordered me to get in quickly as he had a new assignment. As if I needed more on my plate. Yeah, it was getting boring, what with the murder and security cameras and varmints roaming the store.

Tina tried to stop me on the first floor, but I waved her off and made it to the elevator. Foster was nervously drumming on his desk when I entered his office.

"Sit," he commanded. He got up and paced behind his desk, looking out onto Hennepin for a bit. "I've made a decision here that's going to affect you, Biersovich."

My interest was piqued. The initial thought was I was being released of some of my duties in order to concentrate more fully on one, either the murder or store security. My guessing accuracy had been taking a beating lately, however, so the thought quickly passed.

"We have some situations at the store that call for swift action," he continued. "Jane's death has left us in a particularly difficult position. The issues that she normally would deal with have been left hanging. For that reason, the board has decided to name an interim director of facility planning. I trust this development won't interfere with your ongoing duties."

"I can work with anyone, sir. Who is it?"

He paused and looked out the window again before responding. "You, Mr. Biersovich."

I've often heard the expression you could have knocked me over with a feather and not fully understood it. Now I did. My brain was having a hard time parsing the impact of those words.

"You can continue to work from your present office, or you can move into the executive suite, your choice. But I would recommend you move up here. There will be quite a bit of interaction with the rest of the team." He paused to wait for some sort of response. When I continued to stare blankly, he said, "Is there a problem? Do you think you can fulfill your duties?"

"No. I..." The continuation of my response was interrupted as I pondered the options: Can't? Won't? Am not qualified?

As I struggled to regain my tongue, another person entered the office behind me.

"You called me, Mr. Foster?" It was Bambi Schroeder, the fashion buyer who had once served as my assistant on a previous occasion.

"Yes, Ms. Schroeder. You will be working with Mr. Biersovich."

"But what about—"

"This is a temporary assignment," Foster interrupted. "We need to get back up to speed on some items, and you and Mr. Biersovich will serve in that capacity. This is a direct order from Mr. Scalabrino." I glanced at Bambi, and she seemed as dumbstruck as I felt.

"Candace will get you squared away. See her for details," he said. He turned back to the window, our signal for dismissal. I looked at Bambi. She was shaking her head. I shrugged, then went to the outer office to consult with Candace.

"Why...why..." Bambi was struggling to form a question. Her brain obviously was as befuddled as mine, although Candace's straightforward litany of items to attend to and logistics for taking over the office somewhat sobered me up. By the time I left the suite with Bambi in my wake and a four-page action list in hand, Candace had arranged for the maintenance department to get me squared away in my new digs by the next day.

"What the hell is going on?" was Bambi's first question after plopping down on Lena's chair in my office.

"I wish I knew," I told her. "We just have to hang in there for a bit until things settle down."

"But I've got a big spring fashion show coming up—"

"Bambi, just take it a day at a time. Remember when we had to do that Santa duty?" Tactical mistake. I suddenly recalled how excruciating that experience was for her.

"If you abuse me again like that, I'll..." She didn't finish, just got up and left.

The light on my desk phone was blinking, so I listened to my message. It was Freddie: "Sorry about that, buddy. Lost my pants. I'll catch up with you later."

Didn't make sense. Some people have Kodak moments. I have "What the hell, Freddie?" moments. This was one of them.

I figured it was another Freddie-an slip, where his subconscious made him say something ridiculous when he meant to say something else.

It was Freddie, so no telling whether he really misspoke. But why was he apologizing to me? I was the one who abandoned him. And what did his pants have to do with it? I made a note to call him at the end of the day. His message was bizarre, but I had bigger mysteries to solve.

18

O ne of the top priority items delegated to me was to contact the city engineering office and try to speed up the street construction project. The traffic tie-ups were hurting business; revenue was off. The head of sales was pressuring Foster to get something done. Of course, that had been offloaded to me.

Candace had suggested the legal department should be brought into the fray to try to goose the action. Threaten a suit and you usually get someone's attention—that was the thinking.

Jason Barth was Foster's attack dog. Whenever he needed to put the fear of God in someone, he sicced Barth on him. A contract expert and seasoned litigator, he was the kind of attorney you didn't want to mess with.

When I called him, Barth didn't know anything about the situation except that the excavation had "effed up" his commute. He was more than willing to engage in hand-to-hand combat with the city's lawyers. He was free in the morning and said he would meet me at city hall at 10 a.m.

Some of the other items on what I came to call "Jane's List" had me baffled. Apparently, there was an OSHA mandate to change out all the exit signs with bigger and brighter ones, plus have some counters moved to increase the width of aisles.

The store was also on a deadline to upgrade the sprinkler system, which had been found to be substandard by the fire marshal. The preferred contractor, the one with the lowest bid, was too busy and couldn't meet the deadline, so Jane apparently had been in negotiations with another installer. But she had been killed before the deal was finalized.

I was only on the second page of the list, and my head was pounding. Now I understood why Jane got the big bucks. There was so much nitpicky crap to attend to, it's a wonder she didn't go loony-tunes berserk.

WHILE I WAS EATING a sandwich in the break room, Lena walked in, folded her arms and stared at me.

"Hi, Lena."

"When ya gonna tell me 'bout Bambi?" she asked with a sneer.

"I just found out about this myself."

"So, I guess I'm off da team."

"Lena, I have no idea what this job entails. It's temporary, just to cover Jane's duties until...I don't know when."

"Temporary got a way of becomin' permanent, ya know."

"Won't happen. I'll quit first," I assured her.

"Don't mattah. When I'm helpin' you, I ain't gettin' commission."

She had a point. As the top jewelry saleswoman, Lena made a sizable portion of her take-home pay in commission. She only gave me an hour or two on a weekly basis, usually in the form of computer services. But I didn't want to lose her as part of my informal crew of in-store sleuths.

"By da way, funeral is Saddiday. You goin'?"

"Yeah, I guess I'd better."

Lena left, and when I looked back at my sandwich, there was an ant crawling on it. I flicked it off and made a mental note to push the exterminator to the top of Jane's List.

Bambi came in for a cup of coffee. "Your phone rang while I was bringing over some files. Someone named Peter Templeton reminding you about tomorrow."

"Templeton?" Name didn't ring a bell.

"Something about cameras?"

"Oh, shit. Forgot all about that. They're coming in tomorrow to install security cameras around the store. You'll have to handle that."

"Me? What am I supposed to do?"

"Just follow them around and get any information they have on the monitoring system and so on. They'll be setting that up in a closet on nine."

"Look, I have a real job. I don't know anything about cameras or the building in general. I know fashion. That's it. I'm only helping you because Mr. Foster said to do it, but I'm not going to get involved in stuff I know nothing about. That's your job." Bambi turned and left.

So I couldn't really depend on her for assistance. Great. Maybe I should tell Foster she doesn't want to play on the team. But that might get her fired. Don't want that to happen. Bambi is pretty good at what she does.

There was only one solution—get my unofficial assistants to fill in where needed. Lena and Tina would have to handle the camera install and pest control while I was observing the legal showdown at city hall.

Tina seemed like the logical choice for the video security system, seeing as she had a recent background in law enforcement. I had barely gotten the words out of my mouth before she agreed to it. She was tired of swatting insects while trying to apply rouge and ready for a break from the cosmetics counter.

Lena, however, wanted nothing to do with the bug men. Sure, she wanted the varmints eradicated, but she didn't want to deal with the exterminators. "Dat crap dey spray ain't good fa ya complexion."

My answer walked into my office later that afternoon.

"Dude, so you're moving after all." Bradley was sizing up the meager furnishings in my office. "We'll get this stuff over there before you collect your first fat check."

"There won't be any fat check," I replied. "And I need you to do something else for me, Bradley." It didn't take much convincing.

"Bro, I was almost an entomologist," he said.

"I thought you were a high school dropout?"

"No. Well, yeah. I didn't graduate. Had a little disagreement with the principal over a keg party at the start of senior year. Anyway, if I had gone to college, I would have studied insects and shit. Got a cousin who's an expert on gophers. He didn't go to the U of M, though. I think he went to Wisconsin. Go figure. Insects and gophers got a lot in common. They live underground and...uh..."

Listening to Bradley jabber, my skull began to pound again. I managed to usher him out, close the door and put my head on my desk. My second headache and the day wasn't over yet. Somehow I survived till quitting time.

My last task was switching jobs for Tina and Bradley. It's not that I didn't trust him to supervise the exterminator's work. Well, yeah, maybe it was. Tina had her fill of insects, however, and threw it back to me.

19

There was an unexpected knock at my door as I was poring through the unsorted golden oldies in my spare bedroom.

When I opened it, Freddie rushed in, headed for the kitchen. "What does a man have to do to get a beer around here?" He found one, popped the cap and started guzzling.

"Freddie, what the hell, dude? Where have you been? And what's the deal with the pants?"

"Long story. Let me get a little more of this in me..." He just about drained the bottle. "Better. Well, sit yourself down because I've got quite a tale."

"When did you get back? Where did you go off to? I came looking for you—"

"Hold your water, bro. I'll get there." He finished off the brew, released a killer belch, grabbed a new bottle, then situated himself in the stuffed chair adjacent to my sofa.

"Obviously, you got back from Indiana some sort of way—"

"Patience, my man. Let me start at the top. You remember when you went off to the drugstore, and I was checking out of the motel?"

I'm sure I blushed because I recalled how I had abandoned Freddie to visit Emmie alone. "About that, Freddie..."

"So I checked out and everything, and I was waiting for you to come back. I guess it took longer than you thought because I was waiting around there for a half-hour or so. I tried to call you, but I guess you were already on your phone or something.

"Anyway, this guy pulls up in a pickup while I'm waiting outside the office. Says he needs some help getting his tractor out of a ditch. I didn't really want to leave, but the fellow looked like he was desperate for assistance."

"I can't believe you got in a vehicle with a stranger."

"Just trying to be the good Samaritan, Beers. So he drives for a while. Not sure which way we went, but it was into the countryside a ways, maybe about 20 minutes from the motel. Then he pulls into a gravel road between a couple of fields, and we go down this road a bit..."

"Sounds like 'Deliverance' to me."

"Nothing like that. Well, almost nothing. So he stops by this field, and I'm looking around for a tractor and didn't see one. 'Where's the tractor?' I ask him. 'Behind those cornstalks,' he says. So we get out of the truck and walk into this field, and I'm still not seeing a tractor or anything. Then he says he needs my pants."

"What?! Needs your pants? How did he say it?"

"'Man, I need your pants.' I thought he was joking, but he seemed serious so I thought, well, OK, you can have them if you really need them."

" 'Deliverance.' Just as I thought."

"No, dude. Just listen."

"Did he pull a gun on you? Or a knife?"

"Nothing of the sort. So I give him my pants. I figure it has something to do with getting the tractor unstuck, even though I didn't see it. Then he says he needs the shoes too. It was those old deck shoes, pretty beat up. But he wanted 'em, so I handed 'em over."

"Freddie, you're a dumbass."

"That hurts, Beers. I was just trying to help someone in need."

"You mean a thief."

"Well, I didn't know that."

"So what happens next?"

"He takes the pants and shoes and tells me to wait, and he'll be back in a bit and we'll take care of the tractor. So I waited."

I just shook my head.

"The guy seemed honest, Beers. I like to think most people are decent and honest."

"Most honest people don't ask you to take your pants off in a cornfield," I replied.

"Irregardless—"

"I told you that's not a word."

"Whatever! So I wait around a while, and the guy never comes back, and I'm thinking he's got some new problem that's taking a lot longer than he thought."

"Freddie, why didn't you realize you had been robbed? Why didn't you call me?"

He shrugged. "My phone was in my pants."

Freddie's naiveté, or maybe just stupidity, was flabbergasting. I was speechless.

"I walked out to the main road and tried to flag down a ride."

"You got some pants out of your suitcase, I hope."

"He had my suitcase in the truck when he left."

"So you were standing out there in your underwear, looking for somebody to pick you up? Come on."

"No, I had tied my shirt around my waist. This elderly lady stopped and asked for directions. I convinced her that I wasn't a pervert—no snide remarks from you—and she agreed to give me a ride."

"So you went back to the motel—"

"No, I figured I'd just go on to Emmie's house, because that's where you were going. I figured you'd go there when you found out I wasn't waiting at the motel."

"Freddie, I've got something to confess..."

"Hold on. So this nice lady takes me down to Shelbyville, which turns out wasn't that far from where the guy left me, and a guy at a gas station tells her how to get to the Slaytons' house."

"You saw Emmie?"

"Yeah. She let me in, gave me a pair of her brother's pants and even lent me money for a bus ticket out of Indianapolis."

This was devastating news. Emmie wouldn't talk to me, but she went out of her way to help Freddie.

"So what did she say?"

"She isn't coming back, friend. I tried. She wouldn't say why."

As I suspected. "Freddie, there's something I have to tell you..." How to explain that I abandoned him and went off to see Emmie without his interference.

"Yeah, what?"

I debated for a few seconds more, but just couldn't do it. "There's more beer in the fridge," I said.

"Excellent! You want one?" He headed to the kitchen for a refresher.

20

Other events were occurring at this time, but they seemed minor in retrospect. Several people quit immediately following 9/11. The trauma level was high, and some folks just couldn't take it anymore. They were afraid to leave their homes.

Mysterious packages arrived in the business office. One time the bomb squad was called. It turned out to be a repaired toaster returned by the manufacturer. A drug-sniffing dog was brought in at one point, but he barked so much he got a quick pink slip.

Before leaving for city hall that morning, I supervised as Bradley and a newly hired assistant moved my gear down the hall. There was precious little to relocate, seeing as there was already a desk in Jane's office. It was just my filing cabinet and some stuff in the desk drawers, plus my Rolling Stones trash can emblazoned with a big tongue. Couldn't leave that behind.

I briefed Bradley on the camera installation and told him to just observe. And call me if any questions arose. I left feeling confident that things were in hand.

Did I mention how often I get things wrong?

Jason Barth and I were waiting outside the clerk's office for the city attorney to show up. We were told he was attending to important city business, which probably meant he was indisposed in the men's room.

Joe T called to summon me to the mansion. I explained that I was busy at the moment but would come when I could. The city attorney finally showed up, and we were walking to his office when my phone rang again. Bradley sounded frantic.

"Dude, all hell's breaking loose!"

"What's going on, Bradley?"

"You'd better get back here, like pronto. The rats are going apeshit!"

"Whoa, slow down. Tell me what's happening."

He took a deep breath. "I was going around with the camera boys, and they had just put up the second one on the third floor when I got a call from Don."

"Don Anderson?" Don is the head of maintenance, Bradley's boss.

"Yeah. He said there was a big hole in the wall, and the rats were pouring in, and I needed to get down there and help clean up. So I go—"

"Hold on! Hole in the wall?"

"Construction crew broke through in the basement. Broke a water line too. Water's pouring out, not coming in the basement yet but they're trying to get it shut off. Then out come the rats—"

"Call the exterminator. I'll be there as quick as I can."

"Which one?"

I wasn't sure when the exterminator was set to show up. I hadn't actually told Tina to schedule it. "I don't know! Any one! Just get one!"

When I hung up, Barth asked, "What was that?"

"There was a cave-in. Construction crew broke through one of our walls in the basement."

Barth turned to the city attorney and said, "You see? This is what I'm talking about, Rich."

"I think I'd better get back there," I said. Barth agreed and asked for a full report when I arrived. He would handle the legal end.

On the way back, Lena called to say she had seen big cockroaches crossing the floor. "I'm from Noo Awlins an' I know roaches," she added. This was the first time she had ever seen a roach since she moved to the Twin Cities, and she wasn't happy about it.

I assured her an exterminator was on the case, and the roaches would be vanquished. Did I mention how wrong I am sometimes?

As I feared, the scene at the store was chaos. The process of retail merchandizing had ground to a halt on the first floor, which was mostly devoid of customers. Clerks were huddled near a register in sportswear, and the cosmetics counter was vacant. No sign of Tina.

I took the stairs down to the basement. In a corner of the maintenance department, there was a gaping hole in the wall and debris scattered across the floor. Don Anderson was on the phone, and the maintenance intern was busily cleaning up as best he could.

When I peered through the hole, I saw a couple of workmen welding a section of pipe. Sun streamed in through the hole in the street above. A puddle of water covered the workers' boots.

Anderson ended his call. "What the hell happened here?" I asked.

"These bozos they send out to work on the streets!" He shook his head. "Cut through the main with a backhoe, then knocked into the retaining wall. Guy must have been high on PCP or something!"

"What's our damage?"

"Besides the wall? Not much. But they opened up a nice little escape route for the rats. Came streaming out of there when the water rose. I've gotten calls all the way up to five. They're running all over the store now."

"I asked Bradley to call an exterminator."

"You did what?!" He shook his head again, then picked up the phone and dialed. "Cubby? Don Anderson...yeah...get your butt down here pronto...I don't care, we got rats, we got roaches, we got ants, no telling what else...no, NOW!" he screamed and slammed down the phone. "Sonofabitch."

"But Bradley—"

"Didn't you have Bradley following those camera installers around?" Anderson asked. "That's what he told me he was doing when I called him down here."

"Yes, but—"

"You do realize he's got a single brain cell, don't you?" Anderson shook his head and walked away.

21

The nightmare continued unabated that afternoon. While Bradley followed the camera installers around, I was glued to the hip of the exterminator, who turned out to be an Eastern European who spoke broken English. If I told him once, I told him 50 times not to spray the merchandise. I knew an emergency inventory count would be in order.

Joe T called again to summon me to the mansion, but I managed to convince him I was needed at the store. He sounded very worried at the latest developments. I said I would be happy to accept any help he could offer.

Freddie called to warn me that the Herald was sending reporters and photographers to cover "the La Scala crisis," as the news side had dubbed it. When I rang to inform Jason Barth of this, I only got his voicemail.

Salmon Foster, however, had a game plan—don't let them in the store. I asked how that could be accomplished. He said think of a way.

I found Tina hanging with other clerks outside cosmetics on the main floor. She was refusing to return to her station until the coast was clear. Chemicals put down by the bug man had caused a frenzy of insect activity as they tried to escape the poison. They were slowly dying, she said, but some were still coming out to play. Besides, customers were practically nonexistent, she added.

She said she would be happy to alert me the moment she saw a photographer enter the front doors. Shouldn't be too hard to spot with the dearth of customers.

"What's with all the security cameras?" she asked. "We going to be on 'Candid Camera' or something?"

I glanced around the ceiling and noticed there seemed to be more cameras than necessary to cover the first floor. I counted nine in all. Perhaps just because the first floor gets the most traffic, I reasoned.

But when I went up a level, there were another eight. At that rate, the store would contain far more than the 52 originally agreed upon. Were the installers taking advantage of Bradley's cluelessness to jack up the cost of the project? Had to locate them and find out.

Bradley had called from three so I went up to four. Already done. Another eight cameras. I found them on five. Two guys were hanging a support in the far corner of the watch department. One was on a ladder while the other was assembling something from parts on a cart. Bradley was leaning against the wall, bobbing his head to sound coming through the headphones he was wearing.

"What's the deal with the cameras?" I asked the guy working at the cart.

"Sorry?" he replied.

"I'm Jim Biersovich, head of security for La Scala. When I contracted for this setup, I was told there would be 52 cameras in the store. It looks like you're putting in way more than that. We're not paying for this."

"Well," he replied, "I don't know about that. I was told to cover each floor. We're just installing what's needed to see the blind spots."

"What blind spots?" I asked, looking around the floor.

"You've got some supporting columns that obstruct the view," he replied, pointing across the room. "If we don't put cameras at all the cross points, you'll miss some spots." He shrugged.

"But they told me 52—"

"That was on the estimate, right? You did see the part about contingency for line of sight, right?"

I didn't remember anything on the contract about that, but then again I wasn't a contract expert and hadn't looked at the fine print all that closely. I took the guy's word for it. Foster is going to shit a brick when he finds out the cost is escalating, I thought.

Finding the contract and huddling with Jason Barth were imperative. He was the guru on legal documents. If anything could be done, he would find a way, I reasoned.

When I reached the ninth floor, I instinctively headed down the corridor to my office. It wasn't until I walked in and saw it cleared of all but my desk that I remembered I had been relocated.

Bambi was sitting in Emmie's chair when I arrived at Jane's old office. She had a sour expression, like she was being punished and couldn't wait to be let out for recess.

"Hey, Bambi, anything going on?"

"I don't have time for this crap," she responded. "The phone's been ringing off the hook. I'm missing my trunk show. This isn't what I signed up for!"

"OK, OK. I'm not happy about this either. Just give me my messages and I'll get on them."

"What messages?" she replied. "I told them to call back."

Good grief. Exhibit A that Bambi wasn't going to make it as a secretary, even in the short run. I could ask her to help me look through the files, but what was the point? She would do it half-assed and just slow me down.

I went in the inner office and closed the door. After a few minutes of contemplating Jane's chair, I sat down and looked around. My filing cabinet had shown up, thrown in the corner at an angle. Jane's computer was on the credenza, awaiting login. There were three filing cabinets lined up on the left wall, presumably containing all the pertinent data I would need to peruse.

The light on the desk phone was blinking. I picked up the handset but had no clue what number to dial for voicemail, so I replaced it.

Almost immediately, it rang. It was Foster.

"Come see me," he summoned.

22

W"e have a situation," he said after I entered his office.

"Sir, we've got a shitload of situations, pardon my French."

"This one takes precedence," he said. "With everything going on, we need to stay on course."

"I'm not certain what you're talking about."

"PR, Biersovich. If anyone from outside La Scala contacts you, the situation is under control, and it's business as usual. That's what you're to say."

"Regarding what?"

"Anything! Everything! We can't let some minor setbacks impact sales. There's too much at stake."

"Mr. Foster, with all due respect, I don't see how we can keep the Herald's reporters out of the store—"

"Wait now. I didn't say anything about Herald reporters."

"I've been told they're on their way over. They'll probably want to speak with you."

"There will be no story. Don't even let them in."

"Sir, how do you propose to keep them out?"

"You used to work at the paper," Foster said. "You know who the reporters are. Meet them at the entrance—"

"I don't know who they are. I haven't worked there in a couple of years. They may have a whole new staff. And there are student interns in the fall. And besides, we have multiple ways to enter the store. I can't cover them all."

"Well, figure out a way. We don't need any bad publicity with Brand X breathing down our throat. The enemy is at the gates.

Now get on it." With that, he strode briskly out of his office, leaving me confounded once again.

As I was leaving, I told his secretary, Candace, that Foster had mentioned "Brand X," and I didn't have a clue what that was.

"Oh, you know." She whispered, "That other department store that starts with 'D.' We don't mention them by name."

So Foster thought the competitor was launching an attack in La Scala's hour of crisis. The old kick 'em when they're down routine, I guess.

Bambi had abandoned her post when I returned to my new office. If I was supposed to keep newspaper folks out of the store, I would have to cover both the main entrance and the skyway access portals on the second floor, an impossible task.

On the other hand, since the store was mostly devoid of customers due to the bug invasion—word of mouth must have spread pretty quickly on that one—it might be easy to spot a reporter snooping around and grilling employees.

Lena and Tina were only too happy to man the store entrances on the skyway level. They wanted nothing to do with their departments until the coast was clear, bug-wise. Their bosses raised no objections when I mentioned that the order had come from Foster.

I camped out near the front doors at Hennepin. Lots of folks were passing by on the sidewalk, but few were entering to shop. Just as well. There was enough commotion in La Scala without the added pressure of customers looking for service.

There were a few shoppers, however, who took advantage of the relative vacancy of the store to peruse at leisure. Only once did I hear a yelp and see a shopper scurry for the front door.

I stopped the woman and inquired whether everything was all right. She informed me that she moved a dress on a rack, and a rat fell to the floor. And she would never step foot in the store again.

I got her name and address and said I would be sending a gift certificate, assuring her that the infusion of pests was a result of the city's demolishing the street. There would be no more vermin once the exterminators finished their work. She seemed unconvinced. It was an incident that would require me to fill out some paperwork later.

While keeping my eyes peeled for reporter types, I saw Joe T enter the store. "The boss is waiting for you, Mr. Biersovich," he said. "And he doesn't like to wait."

That went without saying. Johnny Scalabrino was used to getting his way. When your reputation included persistent rumors of mob connections, valid or not, you generally got what you wanted.

I tried to explain the peril besieging Scalabrino's empire, but Joe T wouldn't have it. Get a sub, he said, and get to the mansion within the next 20 minutes. Then he left.

Lacking a choice, I drafted a clerk from sportswear and briefed her on the basics: Look for anyone carrying a notepad or camera, and call me when in doubt.

Getting out of downtown took some doing, what with the maze of street work, but I managed to hit the parkway and pull up in the front drive of the mansion only a few minutes past the commanded deadline. The front door was open, so I walked in and took a seat in Scalabrino's den, where I had been an occasional visitor.

The room was empty. No sign of anyone, but I was certain they knew I had arrived. My thirst buds suddenly sprang to life and without hesitation, I stepped to the side bar and poured some vodka. Middle of a workday, but who cared? If they fired me for drinking on company time, no big loss. I was doing a job I didn't want to do in a place where my girlfriend was absent. What was keeping me there?

The thought of Emmie and her continued shunning of me made me sad. It would be one thing if she just came out and said it was over. But she wouldn't even do that. No communication at all. What the hell was she thinking? I had no idea.

"What are you doing up here?" A voice behind me—Joe T, of course.

"You said to come to the mansion—"

"I told you to go to the basement."

"No, I don't think you did."

"C'mon, let's go." Joe T led the way down a hall to a stairway. It let out to another hallway in the lower level. At the end of the hall was a large room outfitted with exercise equipment. Johnny Scalabrino was sitting in a rowing machine, panting and sweating.

"Mr. Biersovich. So good of you to come," he said. "Report."

23

The sight of Johnny Scalabrino exercising wasn't what I expected. It left me speechless for a few seconds before I did as instructed. When I finished, Scalabrino started rowing. After a minute, he stopped and addressed me.

"Here's what will happen. You will go back to your office. Wait for me there. Together we're going to get a handle on this. Now, I need to finish my routine." And he started rowing again.

Joe T nodded at me to follow him back up the stairs.

"What's going on here?" I asked.

"Johnny had a wake-up call is what," he said. "He's getting himself back in shape. These are hard times. You understand?"

I did. On the ride back I considered the ramifications of having Johnny Scalabrino on site, running the show. It was unprecedented, for sure, but hey, it's his store. He can do what he wants. Besides, I was better at taking orders than giving them.

Tina was waiting for me outside the executive suite when I returned.

"You're not at your post," I admonished.

"You've got company," she replied.

"Who?"

"Herald. Waiting in your office."

They weren't exactly in my new office. Lena was standing in the doorway, glaring at a man with a notepad and a woman with a camera around her neck who were sitting in the anteroom chairs.

I introduced myself, then asked them to wait for a second, ushering Lena into the inner office and closing the door.

"Anything happen?" I asked her.

"Dey tried to tawk ta some clerks, but Tina 'n' I ran intahference. Girl shot a pictcha of me—dat was it."

"I may need you to stick around for awhile and help me out. Can you do that?"

She shrugged. "Don't see why not. Not like we got a lotta customahs right now."

I gave Lena the general outline of what I wanted and walked back out to confront the fourth estate.

"Now, what can I help you with?" I asked.

"Carl Potter. I'm on the biz staff at the Herald. This is Genevieve," he said, indicating the photographer, who was already snapping shots of me. "Wondering if you can answer a few questions."

"I'll try." I gave them my shit-eating grin, knowing full well that they weren't going to get anything substantive out of me.

"We understand La Scala is going to be shut down while the investigation proceeds. Can you comment?"

The statement caught me by surprise, and I'm certain my expression made for a telling photo, as Genevieve kept snapping away.

"I'm sorry, could you just...what did you say?"

"The closing of the store. We need some official statement on exactly when and how long the shutdown will be. And if you could provide some numbers on potential lost sales, et cetera..." He sort of smirked when he finished. I wanted to wipe that look off his face with my fist, but somehow my better judgment kicked in.

"I'm sorry. I think you're misinformed," was all I could come up with.

"I don't think so," he retorted.

"No, there's no plan...where did you get this idea that the store is closing?"

"Perhaps I could talk with someone higher up..."

"No. You can't," I said sternly. "La Scala isn't closing. There's no story. I think you'd better look elsewhere for your sensational headline." I gave him the stink-eye.

"Sorry, I guess you're not on the need-to-know list."

"Look, buddy. You're starting to piss me off," I said heatedly. "I'm in the know. In fact, I just talked with the owner not 30 minutes ago. There is no plan to close the store. Get it? Do you understand English?"

He sensed my anger and backed up a step.

"Now...anything else?"

Apparently, there wasn't, because he left, dragging the photographer with him. Behind me, I heard slow clapping and turned to see Lena in the doorway.

"Attaboy, chief," she said.

"Can you follow them and make sure they leave? Don't want them chatting with anyone behind my back."

"Gotcha." Lena caught up with them at the elevator.

It was time I found out what was really going on. I strode past Candace into Foster's office without being announced.

"What's this about the store closing?" I demanded.

Foster regarded me with a surprised expression.

"Closing? Where did you get that?"

"Herald reporter was just here," I said. "Claimed we were being shut down. Something about an investigation."

Foster rubbed his chin, then looked out his window onto Hennepin Avenue. "They want to play hardball, do they?"

"Mr. Scalabrino is on his way up here," I said. That brought him around.

"Scalabrino? How do you know that?"

"I just spoke with him not too long ago. Whatever is really going on around here, you'd better get ready to explain it to him." Foster usually was the one to put the fear in others, but this time the tables had been turned. I headed back to my office three doors down.

There was a song appropriate for this occasion, but it didn't pop into my head until later: "Eve of Destruction."

24

"D ey gone," Lena reported.

"Come back up to nine," I said. "I could use your assistance."

Being thrust into a new role at La Scala had even further addled my inadequate brain. But I was determined to do the legwork necessary to get a handle on things. First order of business: look through the files.

Jane's filing cabinet folders were stuffed with contracts, regulations and other official documents. Lena arrived to find me sitting on the floor surrounded by stacks of paper.

"Whatcha lookin' faw?" she asked, hands on hips.

"First off, I have no idea what Jane was responsible for. I need to know what kinds of things she did, what projects she handled, whom she contracted with, what government agencies she had to contact for various stuff. I need to make a list. Then, somewhere on that list, we'll find the killer."

Lena smirked. "Howya figyah dat?"

"I don't know. It's just a hunch."

"Ya know, dere's a bettah way ta do dat." Lena went to my desk and sat down at the computer. After working at it a few minutes, she announced, "Heah ya go, chief."

I looked at the screen and saw she had opened a file labeled "Contracts." In it were items for various building services—electrical, plumbing, elevator repair, furnace tune-up, pest control and the like. There was another folder labeled "Regulations" and yet another called "Planning."

"Good work, Lena. So can you get me a list—"

"Contractahs, guv'mint agencies...dey all heah. I'll have ya list shawtly." She continued to peck away at the keyboard, so I left her to it. I thought about cleaning up the mess on the floor but decided I needed a break.

"I'm going to run out and pick up some lunch. You want anything?"

"Yeah, get me a walleye sammich," she said. "Some a dem sweet puhtatah fries." She delivered her order without looking up from the screen.

Jason Barth intercepted me at the elevator. "Come with me," he ordered, heading back toward the executive suite.

"I was just going out for lunch—"

"No time," he replied. I followed him into Foster's office.

"Just as you thought, Salmon," Barth began. "Dick is pressing the issue. I don't know who's behind it, but I've got a hunch."

"So do I," Foster replied.

"The building inspector is Jack Padgett. If you recall, he was indicted for malfeasance a few years back, but his lawyer got it thrown out on a technicality. Now he's got his own little lapdog to put the bite on whoever earns him the most political mileage. We seem to be on the menu."

Foster rubbed his chin, then looked toward me. "What does Scalabrino say about this?" he asked.

Since I was clueless about most things at the store, particularly whatever they were talking about, I shrugged. "I have no idea what this is all about or what Mr. Scalabrino thinks. Why don't you ask him when he gets here?"

Barth looked surprised. "You didn't tell me Mr. S was coming up here, Salmon. What does he want?"

"No idea," Foster replied. "Who do you know at the capitol? We need to run interference until we get a handle on this."

After pondering a few seconds, Barth said, "I'll call the governor's secretary. We used to...I know her from back when." He didn't elaborate, just left in a hurry.

"Sir, I'm going through Jane's files—"

"No time for that," Foster said. "Go find out what's going on in the basement. I need an update ASAP."

Popping my head into my new office, I informed Lena that lunch would be delayed for a bit while I completed my mission to the bowels of the building.

"Hey, looka dis first," Lena said. I walked around to where I could see the screen. "Inside a dat planning foldah dere was a file called escalatahs. I was wonderin' why dey nevah put 'em in da stoah. Look at da estimate!"

I looked. Four point three million. Yowzah. Cost prohibitive to retrofit for escalators, I imagined. And that was only to go up to the eighth floor. Executives would still need to take an elevator or stairs to get to nine.

On the way down to the basement, I lamented my complicated position: elevated to a seat of power but still only a gofer for the all-powerful Oz, Foster. And although I was somewhat of a protégé to the owner, Scalabrino, I never quite felt comfortable in that role. He treated me special in some ways, but I was still a peon in the scheme of things.

Don Anderson's crew had constructed a temporary wall in the corner of maintenance to cover the breach. He said the street workers had cleaned up a bit of their mess but still had a ways to go before the utilities were restored completely. The water line that was damaged affected businesses across the street. Thankfully, our water supply was behind the building and thus intact.

Anderson said they discovered something while cleaning up around the broken wall. He took me through a makeshift door into the debris area. Just down the wall from the breach was an old phone panel that had come loose.

"This is actually a door behind this panel," he explained, pulling the segment open. Sure enough, behind the phone panel was a dark doorway, with steps leading down.

"Where does this go?" I asked.

"Subbasement. I had forgotten this was here. The old maintenance foreman told me about this maybe two decades ago. We stopped using this phone panel back in the '80s."

"What's down there?"

Anderson shrugged. "It's got water in it right now. City promises they'll pump it out in a day or two. I would imagine that's where some of our rats are escaping from."

That sent a shiver down my spine. "I hope the exterminator has been through here."

"Haven't noticed, but then again, I've been preoccupied."

"Let me know when that gets pumped out. We need to get him down there and plug any rat holes."

Anderson smirked. "You know they come up through the walls, right? You could seal off the entire basement and we'd still have rats."

That wasn't very good news. With everything else going on, the rats were perhaps the most troubling development. And I was certainly no pied piper.

25

I had just briefed Foster on the status of the basement when Lena dropped a bombshell.

"Headin' out tamorrah."

"What?"

"Goin' home ta Noo Awlins. Be out fa a coupla weeks."

"No, no, no! You can't leave me right now! I need you to help me!"

"No can do. Gotta help my mom. Dad says he's gonna enlist an' go kill some terrahrists. He's too old fa dat."

"Why don't you just call him," I said, "talk some sense into him."

Lena shook her head. "You don't know my old man. He gets an idea, ain't no stoppin' him. I gotta go."

This was yet another item in a growing list of bad news. I didn't have to mentally scan my music collection for long to come up with an appropriate theme—"Same Rain Falls" by Robin Trower:

His world is tumbling around him as he feels the walls closing in...

In this case, walls were actually tumbling. Already I had lost Jane, Emmie and now Lena. The walls of my secure world kept crumbling. I didn't think I could last much longer. "I'm heading to lunch now," I told Lena.

"Don't fuhget my sammich," she replied.

On the way up the street to the deli, my phone rang. Although I was tempted to toss it in a nearby trash receptacle, I answered it.

"Hey, son. How's it going?"

"Fine, Dad. What's up?"

"Well, I've been doing some thinking. I believe I'm going to put my house on the market. Just wanted to let you know."

"Sell the house? But why? You love that place."

"Jim, I have to tell you something. Since Jane died...I don't think I can stay here anymore."

"But that house—"

"Not just the house. I mean here, the Twin Cities. I just don't want to be here anymore. It's not you. Don't get that idea. I just have a feeling of dread every day when I wake up. I can't shake it."

"But...where will you go?" I suspected he would say he would move near one of my siblings, Tom or Jean.

"Florida. Still have lots of friends down there. I've been talking to Watson, my old neighbor. He said there's a place for sale in those townhouses near the golf course, not too far from where we lived. I may go down there and check it out. Police gave me the OK to leave town."

This was another blow to my psyche, on top of all the others. Somehow I had crossed the street and made my way to The Crater, because I found myself sitting at the bar with my head in my hands.

Sam Skejeski, the proprietor, noticed me and delivered his normal greeting: "There he is! Beers, the king of b—hey, whatsamatter, big guy?"

"Everything. Beer me."

"Tell me about it. And what'll ya have?"

"Beer. Cold."

Sam looked at me a bit strangely, I'm sure, because I'm usually very specific in my choice of quaffs. He guessed I was in a hoppy kind of mood and brought a new beer that he called Dogfish Head. Odd name but zippy taste.

I had no desire to recap the events besieging me since that fateful day of 9/11, but Sam has a way of pulling out information by subterfuge. By the time I realized I had brought him up to speed, I had gone through three pints and was feeling somewhat better.

Sam urged me to go home, but I knew I had to go back and face the inevitable.

As I walked back to La Scala, my phone rang. "Where the hell are you and why aren't you answering your phone?" It was Joe T.

"I did answer it, and I'm on my way back to the store."

"I've called six times. Get your ass over here!" He hung up and I checked the phone. Sure enough, I had missed calls—10 in fact. If the phone rang while I was in the pub, I must have tuned it out.

Lena was sitting in Emmie's old desk when I returned.

"Where's my walleye?" she asked.

"Oh, shit! I forgot! Sorry."

"I'm outta heah," she said, getting up to go.

"Wait! Please don't leave. I really need you right now," I pleaded.

A voice behind me said, "Miss Fangeaux, you may leave. Go help your mother." It was Johnny Scalabrino, and behind him was Joe T.

"Thanks, Mistah Ess," she said, departing.

"Mr. Biersovich, we have work to do," Scalabrino said, leading me into the inner office. Joe T took Emmie's station.

Scalabrino sat behind Jane's desk and invited me to sit in the visitor's chair.

"Here's what's going to happen," he began. "You and I are going to clean up these files, get the store in shipshape and make the buying public love us once again."

"But I don't...I need Lena. You can't just let her leave!"

"She has to prevent her father from going off on some wild goose chase."

"But my father is planning to leave, too. He wants to move to Florida."

"There's a big difference—hers wants to go to the Mideast," he replied. "Now, let's just get down to business, shall we?" He pushed a stack of papers across to me and instructed me to start at the top, calling for certain bits of information while he checked against the computer records.

My head was fuzzy from beer and my stomach was empty of real sustenance, but I managed to survive the afternoon and work to the bottom of the stack. Scalabrino seemed pleased at our progress and ordered me to report to work early the next morning—before my three-martini lunch—so my faculties would be sharp.

I doubted "sharp" would be possible.

26

Friday, September 21

The weight of problems on my mind had me staring at the ceiling from my pillow into the wee hours. At some point, Bobby Lewis started crooning "Tossin' and Turnin'" in my imagination.

I was exhausted and ill-prepared for another day at the salt mine, with my only consolation being the impending weekend. In an attempt to stave off drowsiness, I brewed a full pot of coffee and drank all but the dregs.

Something had to give, I determined. Pacing up and down in front of my wall of music, I contemplated my inevitable departure from the world of La Scala. I had tried several times to quit, only to be dragged back in by money or the allure of a glamorous woman. The money meant nothing, and the woman was gone. The only thing keeping me there was the unanswered question: what next?

Perhaps I should follow Dad to Florida, seek employment in a sunnier climate, where the threat of dying on black ice was nonexistent. *And do what there?*, I asked myself. *Set up beach umbrellas? Work in a souvenir shop? Don a Mickey costume at Disney World?*

My prospects, as always, seemed slim. What was I trained for anyway? Journalism, a career designed for people who read and write at a third-grade level. I was perhaps qualified to teach grammar school English.

Or go back to work at a newspaper.

Speaking of the devil, when I checked my phone for messages, there was one from Freddie. He was heading to Chicago Saturday to cover the reopening of the NFL season, Vikings at Bears. Incidentally, he said, a reporter was following up a rumor that one of the 9/11 terrorists trained to be a pilot in the Twin Cities. Just great.

Scalabrino was waiting for me at the elevator when I disembarked on nine. "We have a meeting," he said. "A gentleman from Capital Lease Management is waiting in the inner office."

"What's that?" I asked.

"He has a proposal for us and I'd like you to hear it and make a judgment."

"But I don't—"

"He's waiting. Shall we go?" Scalabrino was insistent, so I had no choice but to go along.

A man wearing an expensive-looking dark suit sat in the chair across from my new desk. He was about Scalabrino's age, with close-cropped gray hair and wire-frame glasses. He stood up as we entered.

"Mr. Sally," Scalabrino said, "this is Jim Biersovich, director of facilities."

"Jake Sally," he said, shaking my hand. We sat.

"As I was explaining to Mr. Scalabrino," Sally said, "what I'm proposing is a lease-back option with declining rate amortization..." He lost me from the first sentence, but as he continued speaking, I somehow gathered that he was offering to buy the building housing La Scala.

When he paused, I spoke. "So let me get this straight—you want to buy our building and manage the property. Is that what I'm hearing?"

"Yes, in a nutshell," he said with a beaming smile.

I glanced at Scalabrino, who had his poker face in place. He was offering no clue as to which way this should go.

My knowledge of financing and property exchange was nil, so I approached it the way I would have when I was a reporter.

"So in layman's terms, you buy the property, we lease it back, you manage it as far as maintenance and so on?"

"That is correct. The terms are quite favorable for La Scala. In the first few years, you gain a considerable infusion of capital as we pay the bulk of the property cost. In year seven, we cross over and you begin paying a minimal management fee and we assume the debt burden. Also, we manage all maintenance and building enhancements utilizing our team of preferred contractors, all A-quality concerns. La Scala would be free to concentrate on selling quality merchandise." He smiled broadly again.

Another glance at Scalabrino told me he wasn't going to help. But I could tell with a proposal of this magnitude there would be many lawyers involved.

"Well, Mr. Sally," I said, rising, "we appreciate you coming in today. We'll run this by the board and gauge their interest in following up, then we'll get back to you."

He seemed a bit crestfallen that we hadn't immediately jumped at his offer but recovered, smiled and shook hands before departing. After he left, Scalabrino raised his eyebrows at me.

"I don't know, sir. I'm no financial whiz, but something seems a little hinky about all that."

"Very good, Mr. Biersovich. Hinky, indeed." He explained that the list of contractors told him the deal wasn't on the up and up. "Those companies have the poorest ratings and are only getting work because they're most likely giving kickbacks to Capital Lease Management. It won't be long before they get discovered for the shysters that they are."

"OK, well, I'm out of my depth here, Mr. Scalabrino. I know nothing about all this. I'm not qualified."

"Oh, you most certainly are, Mr. Biersovich. And call me Johnny." He smiled broadly at me. "Now, I have something you need to look into this afternoon and report back to me. Just make some discreet inquiries. It seems our employees are a bit unhappy and are contemplating a strike."

"A strike? What for?" I didn't have anything to do with the union and contract negotiations, seeing as I was part of management but the lowest tier at that. The only knowledge I had came from Tina, who occasionally complained about the amount of dues extracted from her check. In fact, that was the same gripe I had when I worked at the Herald and was a reluctant member of the Newspaper Guild.

"This is what you're going to find out," Scalabrino replied. "Now, would you like to go to lunch? I'm in the mood for a butter-knife steak."

"Thanks for the offer, but I think I need to grab a bite with a certain La Scala employee if I'm going to find out the information you want."

"Good. Always on the job," Scalabrino replied, extracting a $50 bill from his wallet and pressing it into my palm. "Lunch is on me."

27

Tina was hesitant until I told her I was paying and she could pick the place. She opted for one of the ritzier dining rooms in the skyway. The mâitre d' had no problem with Tina's cosmetics smock but requested that I don one of the available jackets in the restaurant's coatroom.

"You look like a doof," Tina snickered after we had been seated. The burgundy jacket was about four sizes too large and I was tempted to fold back the sleeves.

"Seems like a double standard," I remarked, "what with you in a rouge-smeared uniform."

"Meh," she replied. "So what's the occasion? You springing for lunch is not a normal happenstance. You gonna propose to me or something?" She grinned.

"This is a business lunch, in fact. Scalabrino is worried that you folks are going on strike. What's the story?"

"He must've heard it wrong," Tina said. "Not a strike but maybe a job action. We've had a number of people quit because of conditions in the store. You've got rats and ants crawling over everything and Big Brother watching our every move. The union stewards don't like that very much."

"When you say 'job action,' what exactly does that mean?"

"It could be any number of things. Maybe a sickout one day or informational signs—"

"Signs?"

"Pickets. On the sidewalk in front. The union wants to show some sign of dissatisfaction with the current hostile working environment—"

"Hostile? In what way?"

"It's a war zone, Beers. People are afraid to come to work. You got terrorists blowing up buildings, people getting murdered, insect and rodent infestation, spy cameras, the board of health—"

"Wait, what? Board of health?"

"Oh, maybe you don't know about that yet. Anyway, lots of assaults on people's rights."

"Look, none of this is the fault of the store. And let's get back to that board of health thing."

"I don't know anything about it really. All I heard was a rumor the city was going to send out a team to investigate complaints because some customer claimed she got bitten by a rat."

This was impossible. Things just seemed to keep getting worse. I was convinced the only way out was a walkout—by me. I would need to take some time off to go job hunting. That plan hadn't worked very well the last time I tried it, but now I was desperate. And desperation is a great motivator.

WHEN I RETURNED to the executive suite and marched back into my new office, intent on delivering my resignation speech to Scalabrino, I was confronted with the backside of a quite curvaceous redhead in a tight-fitting blue cat suit who was speaking with the boss. She heard me enter and turned around. I had seen her somewhere previously.

"Mr. Biersovich, you remember Maria?" It suddenly came back to me—Joe T's niece, a blackjack dealer at the Las Vegas casino. She was more gorgeous than I recalled.

I managed to croak a feeble hi before Scalabrino laid out his plan.

"Maria is here to fill in the gaps while we're short-staffed," he said. "She will be your assistant, since I understand your assigned aide isn't cooperating. Maria will help you get a handle on these issues until we get back on an even keel. Questions?"

Again, not the scenario I pictured. Maria Daventi was one of those women who ooze sexuality from every pore. Concentrating in her presence might be difficult. My male instincts told me to ride it out and do what Freddie would do—make a move on her.

But my common sense prevailed, and I launched into resignation speech No. 329. Only a few of those had actually been delivered, but this one had the impetus of desperation backing it up.

When I finished, Maria smiled and looked at the boss, who maintained a poker face. I waited a good minute for his response.

"Mr. Biersovich, I accept."

The words stunned me. I was anticipating a dismissal of my carefully reasoned arguments and a counter offer that made it impossible to walk away. But too much had happened, including the loss of my true love, whose status still baffled me.

"On one condition," Scalabrino said. "You see us through this crisis. When we have restored La Scala to normal operations, I will have a nice bonus as your parting gift. It will give you time and financial support as you seek your next career."

OK, now he got me interested. "Exactly how much time and how much financial support are we talking about?" I asked.

"The figure I'm thinking about should provide for you comfortably for a year. That should be ample time to line up gainful employment."

Now we're talking, I thought. The answer to some of my dilemmas. Guaranteed income for a year while I job hunt? I could go with that.

"Although I hate to see you leave," he continued, "I understand your position. You feel you are not equipped to handle the task at hand. Joseph and I disagree with that assessment. You have proven time and time again that you have the wherewithal to tackle tough assignments and find a solution. That is a valuable commodity indeed, Mr. Biersovich."

"Mr. Scalabrino, with all due respect—"

"Call me Johnny."

"Johnny, sir, I appreciate the offer. Can I think about it?"

"It's a sweet deal," Maria interjected.

She was right. Hang in there a week or so while things settled down and the cops nabbed a killer, then coast for a year. It was too good to be true. Why was I hesitating?

"Take your time and mull it over," Scalabrino said. "Talk with Maria and let me know your answer in the morning." Then he left the office.

"In Vegas, it would be cocktail hour," Maria said. "Can I buy you a drink?"

"I know just the place," I replied.

28

eers! The king of Beers!" Sam's greeting was followed up
with a big smile as he noticed Maria trailing me into The
Crater.

"Hello, young lady," he said. "Welcome to the dingiest
dive in downtown Minneapolis. Sam I am, your proprietor."

Maria smiled at Sam. I gave him the peace sign, aimed a finger
at the tap on the left and found us a corner table. At this time of
day, only the diehards were taking up space.

"Quaint," Maria said as she sat. "Reminds me of one of my
college hangouts, only with less character."

"It's close," I explained. "And Sam provides the only character,
as far as I can see."

"Well, what do you think?"

"About hanging around a while longer? I don't know. I've tried
to quit before and Mr. Scalabrino has sweetened the deal each time.
Really, I'm not qualified to do what he wants me to do."

"You seemed to do OK in Las Vegas," she replied.

"Blind luck. The solution literally fell out of the sky and hit me
on the head. Well, not literally. But just about."

"Sometimes it's better to be lucky...especially in Vegas."

"Here ya go." Sam set the beers down on our table. "Aren't you
gonna introduce me to your friend?"

"Sam, Maria. Maria, Sam."

"My pleasure," Sam said. "And why would you be hanging out
with this low-life sort?"

Maria smiled up at him. I needed to head off Sam's train of
thought, wherever it might be going.

"Maria works at La Scala in Las Vegas," I said. "She's here to do some work for the owner."

"I see," Sam said.

No, you couldn't possibly, I thought. "We need to discuss business so..."

Sam took the hint, bowed slightly and went back to the bar.

Maria lifted her mug to drink, and I noticed for the first time a big rock on her left hand. Married? Or just engaged?

"Johnny wants me to provide whatever assistance you need, so tell me what that might be," she said.

"Well...I don't rightly know." I explained how Jane had been murdered, and I had been thrust into her role without adequate preparation. How the fallout from 9/11 had necessitated changes and how street construction had impacted the store. I didn't even go into the vague threats from the political arena or union because I didn't really understand what was going on.

"So Lena got a start," she said. "I can look at what she put together and see if there are any items we need to follow up. What is being done with the security system? Is it finished?"

"Don't know."

"Does the exterminator have the vermin situation in hand?"

"Uncertain."

"So let's prioritize the list, get a handle on one at a time and bring some stability to the situation."

"Maria, I still haven't decided whether I'm going to stick around. I just don't know if I can do it anymore. My girlfriend left, my dad is moving, I'm in way over my head..."

"Why did your girlfriend leave?" Maria asked, then quickly added, "Sorry, didn't mean to pry."

"No, it's OK." I explained how Emmie had disappeared after discovering Jane's body and how all communication had been cut off inexplicably. It was just another hopeless predicament in a sea of such situations.

I glanced at her left hand again. "So, you engaged?"

"Was," she said, flexing her hand to gaze at the ring. "Married for a while. It didn't work out." I sipped my beer and gave her space to elaborate. "Las Vegas is a place where you can indulge in whatever vice you desire. He happened to pick a vice that...let's just say it was incompatible with our marriage." Maria sighed.

"Sorry to hear that."

"Better to know than not to know, right?" she said with a smile.

We drank awhile in silence before Maria announced she was heading back to the store and hoped I would do the same. I told her I was going to have one more beer and think about it some more.

When she left, Sam trundled over and gave me his wolf grin. I refused to play that game, however, and ordered another round, solo.

The answer to my dilemma failed to reveal itself when the bottom of the mug appeared, however, and I reluctantly walked back to La Scala, still torn on my decision, thanks to Scalabrino's sweetener.

Commerce continued at a slow pace. Tina was filing her nails instead of painting other people's. A clerk next to her was making faces at the security camera aimed at the cosmetics counter. At least they were still on the job and not out on the sidewalk carrying signs.

Normally, I would pass by the jewelry counter on my way up to the ninth floor, but with Lena off work, there was no incentive. The other jewelry salespeople were cardboard backdrops to Lena's big, loud personality.

My new office was vacant when I returned. Perhaps Maria had second thoughts herself and decided Las Vegas was a safer bet. I was peeking at the stack of folders on my desk when she walked in and said, "Oh shit."

Which is never a good prelude to any conversation.

"What now?" I asked.

"I was just talking with Mr. Foster," she said. "I think our troubles are just beginning."

29

Troubles is a mild way of putting the situation. Inspectors from the board of health had arrived at the executive suite, five in total, and confronted Foster. His secretary rang me and told me to get into his office pronto.

The head of the delegation was seated across from Foster. She was wearing a dark suit over a beige blouse, no makeup, and sported a stern look. She appeared to be in her thirties but talked with the voice of authority. The other inspectors, all men in dark suits, flanked her.

Foster waved me over to the side of his desk, where I stood and listened to the ultimatum delivered by Madame Inspector. Either the store shut down for a total inspection, or the owner would be subject to a $50,000 per day fine until the building was deemed in compliance.

It seemed a bit extreme to me. Foster was red in the face and looked like he was about to blow. I could tell he was weighing the cost of the fine against the lost revenue of a potential closure for a day or even a few days.

"Exactly what is the purpose of this?" he managed to inquire, once he had gotten his voice under control.

"We've had complaints," the woman said, "from both customers and employees. Unsafe working conditions compounded by intrusion of possibly contaminated water and pest infestation."

"That's preposterous! We have full—"

"It's not optional, Mr. Foster," she continued. "Once the complaint is recorded, the law is very clear. Even if the merits of the complaint are later found invalid, an inspection is required, followed by remediation—"

"Who's behind this?" Foster asked.

"I'm afraid we can't reveal that due to the provisions of the whistleblower law."

Foster's face got redder, and I was certain he was about to launch into a tirade that would have shredded the skin off the visitors. But the woman rose and extracted a stack of documents from a satchel. She placed them on his desk, along with a business card. "You have until 5 p.m. today to give me your answer. Inspectors will be here early Monday morning." Then she led her contingent out of the office, leaving me alone in Foster's blast range.

I was afraid to move, let alone ask what we should do. Foster spun his chair around to look out onto Hennepin Avenue, which may have been what I would have done. Sometimes the universe has an answer written in the sky. But most times not.

"Biersovich," he said in a calm voice, not turning to look at me, "call Mr. Scalabrino and ask what he wants to do. Take the papers with you." He leaned over and put his head in his hands, which I took as my cue and left.

Maria said she was afraid something like this would happen. I asked her what she thought Scalabrino would say. She shrugged.

This is where I left my horse, I thought. Thrust into the middle of a no-win situation, incapable of effectively resolving a problem. In this case, I was a mere go-between, powerless to make a decision but commanded to implement whatever action plan was deemed necessary.

I phoned Joe T and told him I was driving out to the mansion. Some news just needed to be delivered in person. Maria wanted to tag along, thank goodness. I was hoping she could carry the load while I shrank into the background.

We drove in silence, providing space for my thought process to work out what I was going to do. By the time I pulled up in the circle in front of the mansion, my decision had been made.

Joe T greeted his niece warmly, then lost his smile when he looked at me. He knew bad news was on the way. I was more afraid of Joe T than Scalabrino, despite the unsubstantiated but persistent rumors of the boss's mob ties.

Although shorter than me, Joe T resembled Gregory Peck with the demeanor of Clint Eastwood in his grittier roles. I, on the other hand, was more of a Don Knotts with the mien of Wally Cox. I would lose handily in a battle of toughness.

Scalabrino again was in the workout room, sweating to the oldies. I was pleased to note his taste of exercise music coincided with mine—hard rock courtesy of the Stones. "Can't Be Seen" was the current selection.

He finished some reps on the leg press, toweled off and rose to greet us.

"Mr. Biersovich, Maria, so good to see you. Would you like something to drink? Joseph, get these youngsters a beverage."

"We're fine," Maria said. "Jim just found out something you need to know."

My tongue wasn't working at the moment, so I handed the papers to Scalabrino. He glanced them over and passed them to Joe T.

"What are we doing about this?" Scalabrino asked.

"Mr. Foster wanted me to ask you," I said.

"And what do you recommend?"

"Sir, with all due respect, I have no idea. In fact, I came here—"

"Call me Johnny."

"Johnny, I've come here to resign my position. Immediately." Joe T shot me a sharp look. "I just can't do it anymore. I'm not equipped to handle this, and it's not fair to you or your employees—"

Scalabrino held up a hand. "You've said this before, Mr. Biersovich. Yet you've always managed to come through for me. No, wait. I have not been disappointed once in your performance. In fact, if I had 10 more like you, I would have no need to even attend board meetings."

"But I—"

"You have my offer. And it still stands." He stared at me a moment. "Do you still want to step aside?"

"Yes, sir, I do."

"So you're giving two weeks notice, is that it?"

Two more weeks? I hadn't thought about that, but I supposed it was only fair. If I wanted to get on with another employer, I would need to leave in good graces. An abrupt walkout might hurt me down the road.

But go I must. There was no other option.

"Yes, sir. I appreciate the opportunity you've given me, but for my own mental health, I need to resign."

Scalabrino looked at Maria. "Can you get up to speed in two weeks time?" he asked.

"Me? I don't know..."

"Talk to your Uncle Joseph. I think he can persuade you to stick around. Meanwhile, here's what we're going to do about this..."

30

Maria was making a valiant attempt at picking my brain for information she would need to carry the torch while setting the wheels in motion for the inspection. I had trouble focusing.

She had agreed to take on all the duties Jane Mertin had been responsible for if I would maintain my old security responsibilities for the final two weeks, advising her as needed. I did not have to make any tough decisions, she assured me.

That seemed fair enough. Pretty generous, in fact. If I could just do what I had been doing, which didn't include contracts and complying with laws and such, I thought I could survive the final days of my employment at La Scala.

As part of our deal, she agreed to sit at Jane's old desk, and I would assume Emmie's position. I guess the universe did have a sense of irony.

The workday extended into the evening for the executive staff on Foster's orders. He summoned me for an update from the boss and I quickly informed him of the new pecking order. He seemed OK with that. I'm certain he was even better with it after later meeting with Maria in his office. He wasn't accustomed to seeing cat suits in the executive suite, especially on such an alluring figure.

Maria dug into her duties with a ferocity I was happy to see. That left me time to contemplate my future, which I decided would include a visit to a job fair set to open next week. Once a potential employer got a look at me and saw the cut of my jib, how could I be denied? Executive material, for sure—in a safer, simpler line of work.

When Maria was summoned to Foster's office, she spent almost an hour there. No doubt Foster was lining her up to be his inside conduit to Scalabrino. And as events unfolded, a decision had been made about the inspection order.

It was early evening when the big powwow occurred. Foster gathered the entire cast of the executive suite into the conference room. It was standing room only and I was relegated to the back wall. Maria was at the table at Foster's side, and he turned it over to her.

She outlined the media blitz that would occur over the weekend, explaining why La Scala would be closed Monday. Customer safety is paramount blah blah blah. La Scala has always put the customer first yada yada yada. Shopping will be carefree and devoid of any concerns about terror attacks...

It was a lot of smoke and mirrors designed to fool the public into thinking that the shutdown was only for their benefit and not to comply with a government mandate.

Foster wanted Lena to be the face of the franchise in commercials scheduled to run during the weekend football games. It was an emergency air time purchase—no telling how much that cost. When I informed him that Lena had gone south, he asked Maria if she would do it, but she declined. Then Foster asked the group to think of a suitable replacement. Several people said Bambi's name, and she was elected by acclamation. I saw her across the room, blushing and smiling.

As I've mentioned in previous reports, Bambi Schroeder, who serves as a buyer when she's not assigned to be my reluctant assistant, is stacked. She looks like a beach bunny would look if there were beaches in Minnesota. The thought of her in a bikini—well, that would be a sight to behold. Suffice to say she is the definition of pulchritudinous.

The meeting adjourned after Foster barked out marching orders to the required parties. Bambi left to get ready for filming, and the marketing crew adjourned to prepare for an all-nighter.

Fortunately, my role was confined to something I could handle—lining up a couple more First Sentinel guards for the big sale to come.

FREDDIE WAS BUSY with high school football, so I would have to entertain myself for the evening. I had just about decided to hit the movie rental store when Maria suggested we go out for a late dinner. I didn't want to seem ungrateful for what she had done to save me from the grueling job I had been assigned, so I agreed and suggested we hit a burger joint. She liked the idea and said she would meet me there.

Best laid plans. When I was exiting my apartment door, Farraday was there to greet me.

"Going somewhere, Biersovich?" he asked.

"As a matter of fact, I have a dinner date," I replied, locking my door.

"No, you don't," he said. "We need to chat."

His demeanor told me he wasn't taking no for an answer, and I didn't have the stamina to fight him. Reluctantly, I unlocked my door and led him into my living room.

"Quite a collection," he said, surveying my wall of sound. He picked an album off the shelf. "Vanilla Fudge. I seem to remember this band. Just remakes of other people's songs, right?"

I nodded.

He replaced it. "So we've run into a brick wall in this investigation," he said. "Although..."

I waited. He continued looking across my shelves.

"Although?" I prompted.

He turned to look at me. "Is there something you want to tell me?"

I was nonplussed. "Tell you? No, I thought you came here to tell me something."

"Perhaps. Maybe I do and maybe I don't."

He was starting to piss me off. "Look, I have a date. Can you get to the point?"

"A date? Interesting. Would it happen to be with that girlfriend of yours?"

"I don't have a girlfriend anymore," I said vehemently, "and anyway, it's none of your business. So if you wouldn't mind..."

"You wouldn't happen to have a grudge against your old boss?"

"What?"

"And maybe you got so mad at her you shot her." Farraday nonchalantly pulled another album off the shelf. I was too stunned to speak. "You own a gun, Biersovich?"

"No. I don't own a gun. And that's a preposterous idea. Jane was my friend. She hired me."

"Even friends have falling outs," he replied. "Most homicides are committed by friends or relatives. Did you know that?"

This line of questioning was bizarre. He was grasping at straws, which indicated he had no real lead in the case. Some detective he was.

"Look, this is stupid and pointless. I have to go. Would you mind?" I raised my hand to indicate the door.

"I'll go," he said, walking that way. He turned and gave me a look that indicated he was keeping me in mind as a suspect. Clueless, I thought.

31

D ude, you might want to come take a look at this."
Bradley called while Maria and I were in the middle of
a Juicy Lucy at a joint in Lowry Hill. I was off-duty and
told him so, but Maria convinced me that we could
continue our "date" after attending to whatever was going on at the
store.

The place was dead quiet since it was after closing time. Bradley
was waiting for us on the ninth floor and escorted us down the hall
to a small room. It was the place where monitors for the security
cameras were set up. I had forgotten about it with everything else
going on.

It was a room the size of a walk-in closet with a desk and one
chair. Above the desk was a grid of monitors, showing views of the
various floors, rotating through locations at 10-second intervals. In
addition, there were cameras aimed at the store entrance and
loading docks at the back. A deck of cards was sitting on the corner
of the desk beside a cardboard box.

Bradley pointed to one of the monitors and pressed a button on
the console on the desk. "Watch this," he said.

The black-and-white screen showed a clerk at the watch counter
waiting on a customer. The clerk was rather hefty, dark-
complexioned and middle-aged. We watched as she opened the
register to take a bill from the customer, made change and handed
it back to the customer, who then left with her package.

Before the clerk closed the register, she glanced to both sides,
then pocketed the bill.

"What the hell!" I exclaimed.

"She stole some money," Bradley said needlessly.

"You have to confront her," Maria said.

"I don't even know who that is," I replied. "She must be a new clerk."

"Did you see anything else?" Maria asked.

"No, I just happened to glance up and see that," he said.

"You spend a lot of time up here?" I asked Bradley. It was after hours, and I didn't even think he was on duty anymore.

"Well, you said you wanted me to learn how this stuff works. I can show you."

"Maybe later. For now, I need you to save that video as evidence."

"Sure." Bradley reached under the desk and pushed a button. I could hear a tape eject. He placed it on the desk and pulled a new tape out of the box, inserted it and said "Voila," handing me the recording. It was some sort of video recorder tape, a bit larger than a music cassette.

"Let me know if you see anything else," I said. Maria and I left. I wasn't sure what Bradley was supposed to be doing for his regular maintenance duties, but that wasn't my problem.

When I invited Maria to my place for a nightcap, I wasn't expecting she would say yes. I tried to remember whether I had cleaned the bathroom lately and made the bed. Probably not, I concluded.

My music collection had a profound effect on her. She was impressed and located some obscure music that even I had forgotten I had.

"The Electric Prunes! Wow! I heard a song by them when my ex was on an oldies kick. Can't remember the title..."

" 'I Had Too Much to Dream Last Night'?" I offered.

"That's it! Play this for me!" she said, holding out the album. I put it on the turntable and Maria started bobbing her head to the tune. She wiggled her hands toward me, and I joined her in dancing around my coffee table and couch. She was laughing and having a great time. So was I.

A bottle of merlot was consumed. Then another was uncorked. In time, we were slow-dancing to "Nights in White Satin."

Somewhere between us an electrical spark occurred, creating a circuit connection that couldn't be broken. We sat on the sofa and talked about work, life, love, sports and music until the wee hours.

I challenged her to close her eyes and describe something in my living room from memory. She did it perfectly.

She challenged me to tie my shoelace one-handed. I did it, not so perfectly.

And somehow the night flew by and when we looked up, it was 5:30 a.m. Rather than being dead tired, I was energized. I could see the same in Maria's eyes.

"Breakfast?" I suggested. "I know this place—"

"Maybe another time," she said with a smile. "I'd better get back and get cleaned up. I'm going in today to work on the files." Reluctantly, I let her leave when her taxi arrived.

The experience made me want to spend more time with Maria, even if it meant going to La Scala on my day off. There was a song on my shelves that seemed appropriate for the occasion, and in moments the Guess Who were singing "Could This Be Love?"

32

Saturday, September 22

After Maria left, my exuberance wore off abruptly and fatigue overcame me. I fell into a deep sleep, dreaming that I was in a movie theater watching a sci-fi film. A strange-looking alien was beckoning me to follow him. Where he was leading me was right into the film, where I was suddenly the center of attention.

Naturally, I was being blamed for something I didn't do, in this case stealing a spaceship and ramming it into a tree. But the spaceship looked just like my car, and I was transported back in time to a high school dance with my then-sweetheart. It was "Zelig" meets "ET" meets "Back to the Future." Typical screwball dream.

A ringing phone awoke me, as it often does. "We have a problem. Can you come in?" It was Maria, so of course I could.

The first clue of the headache to come was a massive traffic jam downtown. A normal five-minute drive to the store was stretched out by a glut of vehicles parked on Hennepin. I wracked my brain to try to recall whether there was some event that would cause such gridlock. Maybe one of the endless series of 10K runs.

After 20 minutes of sitting almost motionless, the phone rang again, and Maria asked where I was. In a parking lot called Hennepin Avenue, I said.

Don't even bother trying to drive to the store, she replied. Just find a spot to park and walk. Somehow I maneuvered into the right lane and managed a turn off Hennepin. Another half-hour had passed before I finally found a spot and walked toward the store from my parking spot 10 blocks away.

A large crowd was gathered on the sidewalk in front of the store and circling the hole in the street, blocking traffic. They were chanting something and police were doing little to move them from the right of way.

I saw someone holding a sign that read "SHUT IT DOWN!" Tina was standing at the edge of the mob and beckoned me over.

"What the hell is going on?" I shouted over the din.

Inside, she mouthed, nodding toward the front doors. We entered the store, where clerks were huddled near the entrance, watching the scene. The first floor seemed devoid of customers.

"Protest," Tina said. "Came out of nowhere. One minute I was doing a lady's nails and the next this group shows up outside and starts all this commotion."

"What are they protesting?"

"Us. They were chanting 'La Scala must close!' Cops are just letting them block the street." She shook her head in disgust.

Maria arrived while we were observing the chaos. "I called Uncle Joe. He's on his way."

"What do we do in the meantime?" I asked.

"Nothing," Maria said. "The police aren't doing shit to stop them. I just hope they don't get violent."

"Tina...they aren't union members, are they?"

"No! Hell no, Beers! I'd be out there with them if this was a union thing. I don't have any idea who these people are or what they want."

"We don't seem to have any customers. They're stopping them from entering the store?" I asked.

"Not stopping per se," Tina said.

"They're telling them they should shop elsewhere because it isn't safe in La Scala," Maria said.

"So this has something to do with those inspectors who were here yesterday," I opined.

"Maybe. It seems that way," Maria said.

"What inspectors?" Tina asked.

"I'll tell you later," I said. "Meanwhile, I'm going to talk with the police and see if we can get the front of the store cleared. There should be a law against blocking access."

"Good luck with all that," Tina replied.

Maria was ordering clerks back to their posts as I headed out to find someone in charge. The nearest officer was standing with his thumbs in his belt at the curb a short way down the sidewalk, watching the street scene.

"Excuse me, officer. Can you tell me who's in charge here?"

He looked at me like I had a gnome growing out the side of my face, then casually pointed across the roadway, where a cluster of officers were chatting among themselves.

I pushed my way through the crowd, skirted the massive hole still blocking half the street and made it across to the other side. The policeman standing at the center of the group bearing the largest circumference and gray eyebrows looked like the head honcho, so I addressed him.

"Sir, I'm Jim Biersovich, head of security at La Scala. Can you tell me when the front of our store and the street will be cleared?"

He stared at me a beat then began to laugh. The other officers joined in. "Move along, son. We've got this under control."

"I don't think you do. As a matter of fact—"

"Move along! Or do you want to be arrested for obstruction?"

Once again, I was flabbergasted. Arrest me? For obstruction? What about the hundreds of people in the street? Weren't they obstructing both traffic and commerce?

The cops were somehow in cahoots with the protesters, and I was ill-equipped to take them all on. That would have to be the job of someone with more clout.

That someone arrived shortly thereafter—Joe T. He had Detective Cuccia at his side, and after a quick powwow with authorities, protesters were herded off our sidewalk and out of the street. A few stragglers continued their demonstration across the way, but most dispersed. Customers had free access to the front doors, but foot traffic was still low.

Joe T stationed Cuccia at the front of the store and invited me to take a ride with him.

"Where to?" I asked.

"Your apartment," he said.

"Well, my car is just a dozen blocks down..."

"Come on."

33

When we arrived at my apartment building, Joe T told me to go up and change. I asked why. Because we're going to a funeral, he said.

I had completely forgotten about Jane's funeral with everything else going on. It seemed like I was attending quite a few of those since I had signed on at La Scala. Just another benefit of employment under Johnny Scalabrino.

Joe T told me to keep my eyes peeled for anything suspicious. He gave me the same song and dance that Farraday had about murder victims and their killers being acquainted. I said I would but didn't know what I was looking for.

In contrast to other recent funerals I had attended, this one was packed. A long line snaked out of the parlor where Jane was in repose. Some were La Scala employees off on weekends, notably secretaries to the bosses.

"Follow me," Joe T whispered, walking up the line to the front, where the family was receiving visitors for the closed-casket wake. I spotted Lex at the start of the reception line, flanked by a guy who had to be his brother, plus a few younger women and an older woman wearing a veil.

Joe T situated us behind Lex and told me to watch, listen and take notes. The stream of people slowly worked its way up the aisle to Lex, who shook hands, hugged some folks and broke down a couple of times. The brother remained stoic and only shook hands, saying very little. The girls to his side were nieces who I learned spent time with "Aunt Jane" during summers and had gone on a memorable Paris vacation with her a few years back.

And the lady at the end of the line was Jane's sister, Kate, who looked a couple of years older and was the mother of the girls. She sniffled throughout as she greeted each person.

Over the course of an hour, several hundred people inched through to offer condolences. Among them were a slew of friends, some who went as far back as grammar school, co-workers from a previous job in a law office, a couple of distant cousins, several former neighbors from Edina, a woman who played soccer with Jane, her dentist, two of her bridesmaids and a college roommate.

By the end of the service, I had 85 pages of notes and writer's cramp. Nowhere among the visitors was anyone who expressed animosity for Jane or confessed to killing her.

Joe T and I spoke with Lex at the finish, asking whether he had any clues about Jane's enemies. He didn't.

He said he was going through her house, but the only thing he could find so far that was halfway suspicious was a series of emails from someone angry about Jane's soccer team. Lex said it seemed pretty minor, but he would print them out and send them to me.

"She also had a weird neighbor," Lex added.

"Weird how?" Joe T asked.

"Not quite right in the head. Used to dump leaves in her back yard and berate her about putting her garbage can too close to his driveway, stuff like that."

"Was he here at the reception?" I asked.

"I don't know. She said his name once but I forgot."

Joe T told me to give him the notes on any neighbors that had gone through the line, and he would follow up with them. I told him I'd type them up and get them to him in the morning.

WHILE I WAS TRANSCRIBING my hieroglyphics that evening over some ale and acid rock, Lena called.

"How ya doin', chief?" she asked.

"Not good. Just marking time," I replied.

"Still plannin' ta quit?" Tina had obviously filled her in on my imminent departure.

"Less than two weeks. I've had enough. I can't take this anymore. I need to get into a calmer, less dangerous line of work."

"I hear dat!"

"How are you doing with your folks?"

"Dey happy ta see me. Dad's cookin' up a pot a gumbo right now. Mom still on me ta get married...y'know, da usual."

"He still going to war?"

"Says he'll stick around as long as I'm heah. Den he's goin' ta enlist. Mom don't want me ta leave, natch."

"I would guess not. How old is he?"

"Fifty-six in July."

"Isn't that a bit old to enter the military? Don't they have age limits or something?"

"Dey should. He talked wit' a recruitah who said he could get a supply job ovah dere—not combat, but he wants ta be where he can help fight da terrahrists."

"So you're not coming back anytime soon, I take it."

"Not until I figyah out how ta change his mind. He got dat Fangeaux stubbornness—can't tell him what ta do. You'd think gettin' shot once would scare him off."

"Shot?"

"Wounded in Nam. Took a bullet ta da hip. Jus' laughs about it now, says he was a 'hippie.' "

Lena sounded good, and it was great to hear her voice. Although I missed her, I could understand that some things are just more important than a job. She was using up the rest of her vacation and would soon have to go on unpaid leave if this thing with her dad was prolonged.

But she was home, back where she grew up in New Orleans. I recalled my college days there, great lunches at restaurants across the city, late nights in the French Quarter, Mardi Gras, Jazz Fest—and sweat. Heat, humidity and sweat. It was a way of life and something that seemed totally foreign now that I was living in the land of the frozen tundra.

34

Sunday, September 23

Normally, the TV in my apartment is firmly situated in the off position. Occasionally, I will catch a ballgame, but there are very few broadcast programs that appeal to me otherwise.

I had turned the television on to catch the Vikings pre-game show. They were playing the Bears at Soldier Field in their first contest following the national tragedy. While I was still in the middle of compiling notes for Joe T, a commercial caught my ear. It was the mention of La Scala that did it.

In the spot, a heavily made up and smiling Bambi Schroeder, dressed in a white, curve-fitting cashmere sweater and pleated skirt, blue high heels, was slowly walking the aisles of the store, speaking into the camera. She was talking about what a calming experience shopping at La Scala was for thousands of women besieged by the struggles of daily life. How she got a feeling that it was her second home, a secure place, an inviting den of the finest goods offered in America.

And so on. It was a minute of smoke and mirrors intended to gloss over any problems the store was currently facing by painting an ideal picture of the shopping experience.

It had appeal to both women, who would identify with the attractiveness of shopping, and men, who couldn't help but notice the way Bambi was put together. If that kind of sensual woman is hanging out at La Scala, the message seemed to say, you guys need to get in here pronto.

The commercial looked pretty effective to me, but time would tell whether the Twin Cities' consumers would buy into it. Not a bad effort considering the production was a rush job.

Conspicuously absent from these scenes were any views of newly installed security cameras, or exterminators chasing vermin, or protesters demanding the store close. No mention of murdered executives or terrorists. No, none of that would be good for business.

The tag at the end of the ad was a note that the store would be closed Monday to prepare for a spectacular sale! One that would be of epic proportions! An event that shouldn't be missed! Again, no hint that inspectors would be scouring the place, looking for violations of whatever applicable safety ordinances.

JOE T CALLED to invite me to lunch at the mansion, a first. He said Johnny wanted to do something nice for me before my departure from his employ. I almost asked if I could bring something. Then I remembered that Scalabrino was a millionaire and probably didn't need a tater tot hot dish to fill out his menu.

When I arrived at the big house off the parkway, I discovered I wasn't the only guest. Not only was Maria there but also Vi Capriola, Scalabrino's wife. I had met her during my trip to London. It was the first time I had seen her at the mansion, and I wondered why she was there.

There were a few other people in attendance, including the long-rumored but never seen wife of Joe T. She didn't look like she went with him. In contrast to his slim figure, Sue Terrazzo was a bit chunkier and a few inches taller to boot. She was boisterous, whereas Joe T was the strong, silent type, speaking only as much as needed to get his point across.

A couple of Scalabrino's assistants filled out the lunch party. I was situated between Vi and Maria, across from Joe T and his wife, with Scalabrino at the head of the table.

The table looked like it was prepared for a seven-course feast, but to my surprise, the chef rolled out a cart with tureens of soup and a large salad bowl. We had a choice of homemade wild rice or cheddar-bacon soup along with Caesar salad mixed tableside. I suspected the light fare had something to do with Scalabrino's new health kick.

As we were tucking into our salads, the boss started speaking.

"I'm so glad to have you all here with me today. I especially want to thank Vi for coming across the pond. Good to have you here, honey." He squeezed her hand.

"I also want to thank Mr. Biersovich for being here. As you know, he has been instrumental in protecting La Scala from a number of sticky situations. We all owe him a debt of gratitude." He smiled broadly at me. I could feel myself blushing.

"Today, unfortunately, we're saying goodbye to Mr. Biersovich. He has served me well for these past few years, but now feels it is time to spread his wings and fly off to another adventure. I am sorry to see him go. But I wish you well...Jim." He raised a glass of sparkling water in toast.

For a second, I was disoriented. It was the only time I could recall that he had addressed me by my first name instead of the formal "Mr. Biersovich." What did it signify?

"Would you like to say a few words?" Scalabrino asked.

I wasn't expecting having to make a speech, so I said simply, "Thank you...thank you."

"This is where we talk you out of it," Vi said, laughing. I wasn't sure whether she was serious, but I smiled wanly and dug into lunch.

35

I was expecting the hard sell from the assembled company, but it turned out to be the opposite. Instead of listing the benefits of staying in the employ of La Scala, Vi, Scalabrino and Maria enumerated the future possibilities for someone of my caliber.

They had a lot more faith in my abilities than I had.

We watched the Vikings lose to the Bears while playing team eight-ball on Scalabrino's blue felt table in his office. Maria turned out to be quite accomplished as a pool player. She confided at one point that her misguided youth had included many hours hanging out with her father, who was somewhat of a hustler. She even did a few trick shots when the games ended.

The commercial played several times during the game, eliciting cries of "There's our girl!" or "Here we go!" from Scalabrino each time it appeared.

As I was leaving, Vi said, "See you in the morning," shook my hand and wandered back inside.

Scalabrino noted my puzzled look and explained. "You normally have two unofficial assistants on whom you rely, correct? Miss Fangeaux and Miss McEntire."

"Yes, I suppose."

"Miss Fangeaux is away at the moment so you don't have her services. And Miss McEntire...well...she's off the clock for the time being."

"What do you mean? Has she been suspended or something?"

"No, nothing like that. It's just that she's in the union, you see. And while we have some...question about what's going on with respect to the rank and file, well, we need to keep her at arm's length from the internal workings of the executive suite." He smiled at me.

"She's not a spy. And she told me the union wasn't planning a strike. Maybe just a job action."

"Regardless. We have to maintain some separation so as not to unduly alarm the union about anything. They sometimes get the wrong notion and, well, things spiral out of control."

"I see."

"So Vi and Maria will assist you for the remainder of your time at La Scala. Let them know if you need anything. Two things must be attended to immediately. First, go over that camera contract with Mr. Barth. There are some discrepancies." He was talking about the additional cameras that no doubt ran up the cost.

"Second, we have an employee to escort out of the building tomorrow due to some questionable practices at the register." The thief. "You and a store guard will need to be on hand when she's arrested. After those are attended to, I would like you to resume your quiet investigation into Ms. Mertin's death." He shook my hand and went back inside.

OK, I thought, I can handle this. It's only for a couple weeks. Less than that, really. I didn't know how effective my new assistants would be at intelligence gathering, but that really wasn't going to be my problem for much longer.

"YOU SEE THIS Bambi commercial? What the fuck is that all about? Call me." Tina's message was one of two on my machine when I returned to my apartment.

The other was from Dad. "Just wanted to let you know I'm heading down to Florida for a couple of days. Going to check out that townhouse. Will be staying with Bill and Karen Watson, if you need to get hold of me. I think you have their number. Flight leaves at 9:30 tomorrow. OK. Well, talk to you later."

Everyone was leaving, for one reason or another. My inner circle was shrinking. First Emmie, then Lena and now Dad. The only one left was Tina. Well, maybe Freddie too. But he was constantly leaving, going out on the road to cover this or that game.

The vision of Dad stepping aboard a flight brought a song into my head, "Leaving on a Jet Plane." One of the verses seemed quite appropriate: *Don't know when I'll be back again.* That was the story with all my folks who had departed. There was little keeping me tethered to the Twin Cities.

With a free afternoon ahead, I figured it was time to get serious about moving on in the job market. I needed to tackle a task I had been putting off—updating my resume. I would have to have one in hand when I went to the job fair.

It took a little while to locate my old resume, which included stops at a handful of newspapers where I failed to earn a Pulitzer for my excellent prose. Now I could add a couple years of security work to my *curriculum vitae*.

The process of explaining my position at La Scala had me stumped for quite a while, however. "Glorified gofer" isn't what a prospective employer wants to see on a resume. I settled on the only slightly exaggerated title "executive assistant to the vice president for facilities." The list of duties was long, however, and constituted an impressive slate—at least to me—by the time I finished.

And I didn't even include the fact that I had solved the case of a head found in a hatbox, or a missing jade bathtub, or several murders in London. Unless I was applying to be a detective, I couldn't see where that would appeal to a future boss.

"Jim Biersovich—not good at much but a passable gumshoe."

36

Monday, September 24

It was odd to see a guard posted outside the front doors of the store. The marketing department had done a rush job on signs. They were huge and plastered in every door and the display windows:

> **MEGA-SALE!**
> **STARTING TUESDAY, SEPT. 25!**
> **THE EVENT OF THE NEW MILLENNIUM!**
> **ONLY AT LA SCALA!**

Some marketing expert must have determined that the use of exclamation points was the determining factor in the success of a sale. How could a customer resist the exclamation point?

A few folks who obviously hadn't caught the TV spots were confused when they were turned away at the door. I later heard that one shopper became vehement and demanded to be let in because it was his day off and he needed to find a suit for a job interview. Buddy, I feel your pain.

Foster pulled me aside as soon as I entered the executive suite.

"Biersovich, the inspectors will be here at 10. You will escort them around the building. Jason will be with you. Take notes."

"But Mr. Foster—"

"No shoplifters to worry about today. Concentrate on getting us through this inspection." He headed into his office.

Maria and Vi weren't in the office yet, so I had little to do but wait for the health squad to arrive. I was standing near the front doors when Tina walked up and asked why she needed to be there if there were no customers to wait on.

"I can't answer that. It's a normal work day for employees," I replied.

"But there's no work to do."

"Go straighten up your counter or something."

"This is ridiculous," Tina said.

She was right. What was the point of clerks manning counters with no customers? They would be mostly standing around for eight hours, collecting pay for nothing. Actually, some of them might be happy about that.

Jason Barth joined my vigil at the door. Whereas he was in his normal sharply creased suit, I had on my usual casual work attire—black jeans and a black Santana T-shirt. Although I was in management, I didn't dress like management. And for some reason I had never been pressed on the issue. The perk of being mostly an invisible behind-the-scenes worker, I suppose.

I told Barth we needed to examine the camera contract, but he said we would worry about that later.

The crew of four inspectors showed up shortly after 10. They informed us they would be spending several hours going over a list of items they briefly showed us. To expedite matters, they wanted to split into teams of two and cover different parts of the store.

Barth and I opposed this but had no choice in the matter. We split up and followed separate duos. His headed off into cosmetics while mine went down the elevator to the basement.

My two guys looked like big dummies, so I immediately dubbed them Mortimer and Snerd in my mind. They examined the boiler and the water supply, along with the makeshift repairs prompted by the wayward street construction. I heard a lot of "Hmmms" and saw a lot of head shaking as they marked things on their checklist, but they had little to tell me.

They demanded to see all the current building certificates of compliance. I had no idea where they might be but guessed they would be somewhere in the bowels of Jane's computer or filing cabinet. I called up to the office, got Maria and told her what was needed. She said she wasn't real familiar with our computer system but would see what she could find out.

That didn't sound very promising. When I needed computer expertise, there was one person I relied on. I rang her number.

"Where y'at, Beers!"

"Hey, Lena, how's it going? Just thought I'd check in with you and see when you think you might be coming back."

"Dunno. Dad was gonna go down ta da recruitin' centah but I tawked him outta dat by sayin' I'd take him ta da racetrack. It's a daily battle down heah!"

"Well, I was just wondering if you might be able to help us. We need to get hold of any certificates La Scala might have for meeting government regulations—"

"Oh, yeah! I ran across doze when I was lookin' fa da contracts. Lemme make a call."

We hung up and I had a good feeling about it. Lena was smart and capable of getting results in the electronic realm.

When I passed along the information that the forms would be available shortly, the inspectors seemed skeptical. They spotted the old phone panel and asked if it was still functional. I said no, it was actually just a door to the subbasement. This caused raised eyebrows and they demanded to see what was down there. I told them I'd have to get the maintenance superintendent and find out if that was possible.

Don Anderson said the water had been pumped out and we could go down, but there were no lights and it would probably smell bad. He found a couple of flashlights we could use and sent Bradley to escort us.

"Dudes, there's a whole lotta nuthin' down there," Bradley told us as we followed the flashlight beam down the steps. The concrete stairs led into a musty-smelling space littered with various bits of trash and the carcass of a long-dead rat. There were still small puddles in spots.

On one wall was a blackboard, along with a paste that looked like the remains of some green and orange chalk. A half-wall sectioned off the part by the stairs, leading to a smaller section in back. On the floor in the corner was an old waterlogged mattress, a metal chair with a bent leg and more scraps of paper, clothing, a discarded toothbrush, a melted candle, a bloated Hardy Boys mystery and a piece of paper tacked to the wall.

I felt a strange vibe, like there was more to the place than what we were seeing. It was only when I examined the mattress in closer detail that the true horror of the site hit me.

37

S omeone was killed here," I said, pointing to the hole in the mattress and the washed-out ring of red surrounding it. I immediately regretted it.

Mortimer and Snerd looked where I was pointing, glanced at each other, then just smiled.

"Right," Mortimer said with a shit-eating grin. "Well, where's the body?"

Already laid to rest, I thought. I figured it would be best not to give them extra ammunition for extending the closing of the store, so I didn't press the issue. But I made a note to return and look for more evidence.

My dummies met up with Barth's dummies on the third floor to compare notes. They huddled for a few minutes, whispering and going over checklists, then split up to resume their tour. My group entered the elevator, so I scooted in with them.

The roof was their destination. I had only been up there once, during a winter storm when Foster asked me to sweep the snow off his satellite dish because he was getting bad reception. I couldn't believe he had his own private dish on the roof, but I figured it was one of the many perks he enjoyed as the head cheese.

The dish was near the rooftop door, fortunately, so I didn't have to get close to the low retaining wall at the roof's edge. My fear of heights would have precluded completing the task if that were the case.

In this instance, the dum-dums went straight to the roof edge and peered over the wall down at Hennepin Avenue. Perhaps they were observing the street work. Or maybe there was some unsafe condition over the side of the precipice. I wouldn't know. I clung to the door frame and awaited their return.

"You OK?" Snerd asked when they re-entered the stairwell down to the ninth floor. He grinned at me like he thought I was some big yellow belly, which I was, but I didn't want to give him the satisfaction.

"Just making sure you didn't get locked out on the roof," I replied, returning his grin. "Wouldn't want that to happen, would we?" Yes, in fact we would.

I GOT THE CALL while we were finishing up in the break room on seven. "This is Quepanzo Gozam. Lena Fangeaux asked me to give you a call." It was one of the tech guys, half of the "Dweep and Kweep" team in the IT department that Lena had relied on for expertise outside her abilities.

"What do you have for me?"

"Only the approved certificates for the building going back four years. I have PDFs I can send you," Kweep said.

"Can you just print them out? I'll come pick them up."

"OK. Do you remember where we are located?"

I did recall that the computer room had been moved from its basement spot adjacent to the maintenance department to a larger area on the ninth floor, far down the back hallway from the executive suite. Fortunate that that was completed before the street crew broke through the wall in the basement. Otherwise, the entire operation may have ground to a halt, seeing as all the cash registers ran off the computer system.

The inspectors didn't want to hang around to collect the paperwork, however. They were eager to return to their office and begin compiling the new violations they claimed the store was committing, although they refused to disclose them to either Barth or me.

They recommended the store remain closed until all items were brought into compliance. Barth said that wasn't going to happen. Some legal mumbo-jumbo was exchanged, and the inspection team departed before any punches were thrown. A guard let them out the front door.

"Now what?" I asked Barth.

"If it's a war they want, it's a war they're going to get," he said, storming off toward the elevators.

One of the idle clerks tugged on my sleeve. "There's a guy tapping on the front door." She pointed that way, and I saw a worker in hard hat and overalls motioning toward me.

Being chief of security, I could unlock the door and see what he wanted.

"You need something?" I asked.

"We need to shut off your water," the guy said. He looked to be a few years older than me, graying at the temples, with a basset hound face and a pencil over his right ear. The nametag on his overalls said Frankie, with a corresponding patch on the other side that said Viking King Construction.

"Why? What's the problem?"

"We need to repair that main line—" He pointed out toward the street. "And your water flow needs to be off."

"But that isn't even our supply line. Ours comes into the back of the store."

"Irregardless, it needs to be off." He stood there defiantly, and I didn't even have the strength to point out his grammatical error.

"How long?"

"Don't know. May be a few days."

"A few days! No, that's impossible. We've got a store to run."

"I'm just the messenger," he replied. "You got a problem with that, take it up with the foreman."

"And who's that?"

"Footie. Over in that building over there." He pointed to the small portable construction office that had been situated in the middle of the street at the edge of the gaping hole. "Go to the john now because it's gonna be shut off in 15 minutes," he added with a smirk.

No bathrooms? Great. This whole place was rapidly going down the tubes, so to speak.

38

Music was blaring in the construction shed as I opened the door. It was an oldie but moldy, "Kick Out the Jams" by MC5. The construction foreman, a lanky guy with the face of a dachshund and "Footie" embroidered on his shirt pocket, was leaning back in his folding chair with his feet crossed on his desk, bobbing his head to the tune.

"Excuse me!" I yelled over the din.

"Yeah?" the guy said without budging from his comfortable position.

"Are you the foreman? Can you turn that down?"

He reached for the dial on the boom box on the shelf behind him and turned it down imperceptibly.

"What's the matter?" he asked.

"I need to speak to you about the water!"

"What?"

"The water! Can you turn that off?"

I could read the reluctance on his face as he switched off the music. He looked none too happy about it.

"We have a problem," I said. "Your guy told us we have to shut off the water."

"Who's that?" he asked.

"Frankie, one of your workers."

"No, I mean whose water?"

"Oh. La Scala." I threw my thumb back over my shoulder in the direction of the store, which was impossible to see behind the closed door.

"We need to make repairs. If he says we gotta shut off the water, we gotta shut off the water."

"But that's not even our water line you're working on," I pleaded. "Our water supply enters at the back of the store, on the back street."

"Pipes are pipes," he replied. "They're all connected." His hand moved forward, veered left, then forward again.

"But can't you close a valve or something? You can't just shut down a store for days."

"Sorry, pal, but work's gotta be done. We don't fix it now, the whole downtown's gonna be out."

I wasn't making any progress here and didn't have the authority to go over his head to whoever was really in charge. Some faceless bureaucrat, no doubt. Time to kick this up the line to a person with clout.

As I left the construction office, I had a weird feeling. I'm not sure where it came from, but I was absolutely certain that "Footie" was dangerous and I shouldn't cross him. Don't ask why I felt that—I didn't know.

Foster went ballistic when he heard the latest. "Those bastards won't get away with this!" he screamed and rushed out of his office. Candace raised her eyebrows at me as I was leaving.

It didn't take long for word to spread. "The toilet won't flush!" Maria exclaimed as she returned to our communal office. Vi looked alarmed and went with her to the powder room before I could explain.

Pretty soon most of the executive suite was huddled in the anteroom, trying to figure out what was happening. Foster wasn't around, so I told them about the shutoff. There were many questions I couldn't answer, most pointedly when water service would be restored.

The exodus began immediately. Secretaries gathered their purses and headed to the elevators. Some didn't wait and instead took the stairs. Phone lines lit up with calls from other floors. I had never witnessed a stampede, but this sure seemed like one.

Don Anderson rang my cell to report there was a sudden drop in water pressure that he was investigating. When I told him the reason, he cursed and said we would need to evacuate immediately. Without water, the chillers would need to be shut down, which meant no air conditioning. He indicated that also would cause an increase in pest activity.

Terrific. The news just kept getting better.

When I relayed the situation to Joe T, he agreed that we would need to send everyone home. Meanwhile, I should stick around until he showed up.

FOSTER AND BARTH were at the front doors looking out when I arrived at the first floor. I caught the tail end of their conversation, which had to do with getting a judge to issue a temporary restraining order. From their grimaces, I could tell it wasn't going well.

"You inform Scalabrino?" Foster asked me. Again, I wondered why I was the go-between. Had he fallen so out of favor that he couldn't even talk to the boss?

"Joe T is on the way," I said.

"Good. Check the store and make sure everybody is out." Knowing Foster as I did, I was sure it was more to prevent shoplifting than to protect store personnel.

My trip through the store, starting at the eighth floor, was spooky. I thought this must be what it's like to be an overnight guard—walking through deserted aisles with no sign of life. At one point I was startled by a sound that must have been a rat scampering across the sixth floor, but I was reluctant to investigate. Go ahead, Mr. Rat, shop till you drop.

39

Naturally, Joe T wanted to confront the construction foreman and I suspect intimidate him into turning the water on again. That plan was foiled when we discovered the work shed was empty. In fact, there was no sign of crew anywhere around the street project.

After uttering several choice expletives, Joe T said I might as well go home. He would have his guys watch the store until the water was restored. As I left, I saw him huddle with Foster and Barth, no doubt trying to figure out how to reopen for the big sale if there were further complications.

With most of the afternoon ahead of me, I decided to catch up on personal matters: planning for the job fair, finding out how Dad was doing in Florida, perhaps even making another stab at salvaging a romance.

I realized I hadn't notified anyone about taking off to go job shopping but didn't think there would be a problem. Scalabrino had pretty much given me his blessing on leaving the flock.

Dad sounded excited about his pending move. He had signed a contingent sale agreement on the townhouse and said he was putting his house on the market when he came back in a couple days.

Lena reported there was no change in her situation. Her father was basically blackmailing her to stay in New Orleans, or he would go to war. She thought he was serious about it. Lena was surprised by the latest turn of events at La Scala but said she was certain I would get everything under control.

"You can't just stay on vacation forever," I told her. "You've got to come back soon, or you're going to lose your job."

"Yeah, well, 'bout dat...I'm thinkin' 'bout quittin' anyway. Dey got an opening at Dillard's an' I'm gonna apply fa it."

"Dillard's?"

"Dupawtment stoah, kinda like La Scala. High-class joint."

"Lena! I can't believe you're not coming back!"

"You oughta get outta dat place yaself, Beers. Come on down ta Noo Awlins. You'd like it heah!"

"Yeah, I spent some time down there..."

"Right! I fuhgot! So yeah, get yaself down heah. It's a pawty all da time!"

Just what I needed—full-time partying. It certainly sounded more attractive than continuing to work at La Scala. In fact, anything sounded better. *Almost* anything—I still didn't see myself returning to newspapering.

I told Lena I'd call her back later in the week—after I attended the job fair. I hoped it would give me some leads on possible future careers, ones not involving crime and the solving thereof.

Then there was Emmie. My ongoing perplexity at her situation was pulling me in opposite directions. I wanted to continue to pursue her, to learn the real reason behind her abrupt exit. At the same time, I felt it was hopeless to persist in seeking resolution. She had made it abundantly clear that she wasn't coming back, which meant our relationship was expendable.

And that was something I just couldn't accept.

What the hell, I thought. May as well give it one last shot. Give her an ultimatum. See if that shook Emmie out of her inert state. At the very least, I could get some closure and put my self-avowed precise logic to work, move on with my life.

No one picked up at her parents' house, and I hung up before leaving a message. Then I reconsidered and dialed again.

"Emmie, this is Jim. I just want to beg you, please, please, call me back. I need to hear from you the real reason you ran away. You know I still care for you. Deeply. But if you don't feel the same anymore, I'll understand. Just let me know, and I'll stop bothering you. OK, that's it then."

I regretted it almost immediately after hanging up. Did I really just say that? I was signing my own death warrant, I knew, but it had to be done, I told myself. Just like the brilliant Mr. Harrison sang, *All things must pass away.*

I felt sick.

I NEEDED a sounding board, and hardly any of my normal support team was around. There was Freddie—he certainly wasn't "normal" in any respect. So he was it by default. He agreed to come over only after assurances that I had an adequate supply of beer and snacks.

Before I could start explaining my problems, Freddie launched into one of his bizarre spiels.

"What is it with the nine-tenths of a cent on gas?" he asked. "I was getting some petrol yesterday and—"

"Petrol?"

"Sorry. I've been saying that ever since our trip to London. Anyway, at the gas station, you know how they have the price posted, and it's like a dollar forty-nine and nine-tenths?"

"Yeah?"

"What about the tenths? You never have to pay a fraction of a cent. Are they just rounding it up and ripping us off for a tenth of a cent on every gallon?"

"Yeah, Freddie, probably."

"Well, we need to do something about that. It's not right."

"There's nothing we can do about it, but that's not why you're here. You're here to help me work through my issues."

After explaining it all to Freddie—the employment crisis, the loss of Emmie, my existential dilemma—the situation sounded hopeless. To me, it seemed I was stuck in a confining box, facing a wall any way I turned.

"Here's what you need to do," Freddie began. "First, quit that store job and come back to the paper. No, wait, hear me out. Number two, let me fix you up with someone. You remember Gidget? I went out with her awhile, but she's more your type."

"You mean she has brain cells?"

"Not funny. Thirdly, you need to lighten up and start enjoying life, Beers. You're not gonna live forever. And you're just wasting your life away fretting about every little thing. Sometimes you just gotta say 'what the fuck' and jump off the cliff."

"To a certain death."

"No, not at all. To a fresh start, new horizons. There's a world of possibilities out there, but you're confining yourself in this little cage you created. You're not letting yourself out to go roam, explore, discover new things."

"Going back to reporting is discovering new things?" I asked.

"Well, at least it gets you out of dealing with stiffs," Freddie retorted.

Good point. Maybe the best he had ever made.

I was just about convinced that he was right when the phone rang.

40

"When were you going to tell me about the dead clerk?"

Joe T's voice was accusatory, like I was the one who had committed some dastardly deed.

"What dead clerk?" I asked.

"The one we found in the subbasement. Get your ass over here." He hung up before I could reply.

"Gotta go, Freddie."

"Another murder?" he asked, eyebrows raised. "What did I tell you?"

"I hate to say this, but you're right." He beamed at that acknowledgment. "But for the next week or so I've got to ride this out. There's a reward for me if I can do that."

"Wanted dead or alive?" he asked.

We agreed to talk later, after I had answered Joe T's summons. Freddie was ready to go to bat for me with both the sports editor and Gidget. I had turned him down so many times in the past that I thought perhaps I should let him have his way this time.

THE BODY had already been removed, and detectives were talking to Joe T's guys when I arrived. "Name is Britnie Culligan. That's what it said on her name tag. Apparently, a new clerk in the watch department. You know her?"

I shook my head. "What did she look like?"

"Large woman. Ruddy complexion. Shot to the head." Joe T cocked his finger and pointed at his right temple. "My guys found her down here. The door to the subbasement was ajar."

Something clicked in my brain. "I think I might have some information on her. Let's go up to nine."

140

I led Joe T to the security monitor office. "I think we caught her on tape. If it's the same woman, she was filmed taking money out of the register."

"So this is the one we fired?"

"Well...no...I hadn't actually got around to handling that, what with everything else going on."

Joe T glared at me. "So now she's dead, thanks to your inaction."

"You're blaming me?" I asked, incredulously.

"Didn't we impress upon you the need to keep us informed of *everything* going on? Mr. Scalabrino doesn't like surprises. You should know that by now. We've had nothing but surprises lately. Let me see the tape."

I ran down to the office and found the tape in the top drawer of Emmie's old desk. After loading it into the machine, I backed it up a minute or so and ran it through for Joe T. He made me repeat that two more times.

"Well?" I asked.

"You could have told us about this when it happened. This could put the store in a bad light."

"I did tell you. So what do you want me to do?"

"Find out why she was stealing from us and why she wound up dead. The cops will be speaking with her family, so you talk to the other clerks. We can't have someone picking off La Scala employees. Bad for business." He gave me a stern look before leaving.

Fortunately, water service had been restored, and I was able to splash some cold water on my face in the men's room. The gaunt visage staring back at me in the mirror looked like it had aged several years in the past couple of weeks. How old would I look before I finally said goodbye to the store?

THERE WAS an audible sigh of relief from Foster when I called to inform him that the water was on again and the store could reopen for the big sale. He wasn't as shocked as I would have guessed when he learned about the dead clerk. I told him I would be on special assignment during the sale.

Within the hour, the store was again teeming with employees setting up signs and special displays. It was almost business as usual.

It was near the end of my workday, although I knew the setup team would continue into the night getting ready. With little to occupy me—the normal team of clerks in the watch department were off—I headed back home to rest my weary self.

THE DREAM that tormented me that night was a familiar one. I had returned to work at the newspaper, an all-too-frequent scenario. Some of my current co-workers at the store were mixed in with the usual sports staff.

But instead of attending to the business of reporting, the Herald had become a TV and computer repair shop. Again I was a fish out of water, lacking the necessary mental tools to accomplish my job. My supervisor was a buddy from high school that I hadn't seen in at least 20 years.

When I woke up, relieved that it was just a dream, I revisited my usual qualms about returning to the daily rag. I was not equipped to handle it. On that score, the dream was spot on.

41

Tuesday, September 25

I was a bit surprised to see the crowd waiting outside the front doors when I arrived for work. Bambi's pitch apparently was quite convincing, as I spotted a fair number of men in the throng. And Barth obviously had come through with a restraining order to prevent closure of the store.

With only a few minutes before La Scala would open, I made straight for the watch department on the fifth floor. Two clerks named Jori and Lorraine were on duty, so I pulled them aside and inquired about their co-worker. At this point, they didn't know she had been killed.

"Britnie has been acting funny lately," Jori said.

"Funny how?"

"She keeps talking about getting protection. 'He's not gonna get me,' she says."

"Do you know who it is?" I asked.

"No, no clue," Jori said.

"I think it's an ex-boyfriend," Lorraine offered.

"I have to tell you that we saw something on the security video."

"What security video?" Lorraine asked.

I pointed at the camera aimed at the watch counter.

"Oh shit!" Jori said. "I knew it!"

"Knew what?"

"She was going to get in trouble," Lorraine explained. "We saw her take money from the register."

"Why didn't you tell someone?" I asked incredulously.

"Not our business," Jori said. "Besides, if we blew the whistle on her, it would be dangerous."

"Dangerous? Why?"

"Because she's dipping in the till...to buy a gun," Jori said.

"I told her she's crazy," Lorraine said, shaking her head.

"She's really scared. Said she needs a gun for protection. This guy, whoever he is, is out to get her. At least that's what she says."

"Is she married?" I asked.

"Was. She has a boyfriend. I saw him in here once," Lorraine said.

"He's some sort of construction worker, I think," Jori added.

"You may want to talk to Holly in bedding," Lorraine said. "She has lunch with her every day."

"Where is Britnie?" Jori asked. "Did she get fired? We're gonna be short-handed today, and it looks like it might be really busy, judging by that crowd outside."

I shrugged. Not my place to deliver the bad news. On the eighth floor, the bedding department was unstaffed. At least there was no one on duty that I could find. After waiting around for a few minutes, I gave up and headed to the office.

Vi and Maria were working side by side on stacks of papers that looked like contracts. Vi had already heard the news from her husband via Joe T. Maria was convinced there was a killer on the payroll that needed to be rooted out. She showed me a small handgun in her purse, a serious violation of company policy, I was certain.

"I'll be roaming the store today to try to find out some information, so I won't be around to help," I reported.

"No big deal," Maria said. "We're getting a handle on the contracts. We've already found some really questionable stuff."

"Like what?"

"Ms. Mertin had signed a consultancy contract then later canceled it," Vi said. "We're trying to find out why."

I told them about the meeting with Capital Lease Management. It wasn't the same company, however, just an individual named Hugh Vinson. They were going to pore through her emails to see if there was any more about it.

The store had opened by the time I reached Tina, who was little help. She was so busy she barely had time to breathe, much less snoop around for information that would assist me. As I left her, a line of women waited to get their discounted mascara and free rouge application. Tina looked pissed.

A return visit to the bedding department proved frustrating. There was still no Holly in sight, not even a clerk on duty. Several customers asked me if I could wait on them, and I had to disappoint them. Crossing over to luggage, I inquired about the dearth of help in bedding.

"No one's over there," an employee named Jeff told me. "I wish they'd show up. I'm tired of getting mattress questions. And I have no clue about thread count!"

This was a problem I was happy to pass along. When I dialed personnel and reported the missing clerk, I was informed that Holly was supposed to be on duty. Could I wait there until another person could be called in? No, I couldn't, sorry, but give me Holly's number, and I'll try to locate her.

Of course, she didn't answer when I called. Maria was able to track down her address in the office directory. Since I couldn't talk with Britnie to find out why she was dipping in the till, maybe Holly could provide a hint.

The front of the store was chaos as I left. The construction crew looked like it had gone out of its way to place obstacles on the sidewalk for customers to dodge. Across the chasm I could see the foreman grinning or maybe gloating. Not far from him were a couple of pickets, holdovers from the big protest, no doubt, carrying "La Scala—Last Calla" signs. Cute, I thought. They don't know Johnny Scalabrino.

42

There was another appointment on my agenda as I left the store—stopping by the job fair for a quick look at my possible futures. The hunt for the missing clerk gave me the cover story I needed to slay both fowl with one pebble, so to speak.

Freddie has an uncanny knack of catching me at the most inopportune times, which is just about any time he calls. He was again urging me to go along with his dating scheme, but I informed him of the latest events that precluded such frivolity.

"You need to put some barricades up around that building," Freddie said.

"What for?"

"So some bozo with a van full of explosives doesn't ram the store. You'd be one crispy critter if that happened."

"This magical van is going to somehow fly over the Grand Canyon in the street outside and blow up La Scala."

"Well, one day that hole won't be there. They're going to get it fixed."

"At the rate they're going, I'll be long retired by then," I retorted.

"Or shot to death. Man, you got to get out of that place. I'm telling you—"

"I know, I know. I'm heading over to the job fair in a bit."

"Job fair? You shitting me? You're not going to find a job at a job fair," Freddie said. "You need to use your contacts. That's the only way anyone gets hired nowadays."

"True."

"I'm your contact, Beers. And I have just the job for you. They're looking for a beat writer for the Thunder."

"The soccer team? I don't know anything about soccer."

"It seems to me that you told me your soccer expertise got you your current gig."

"I never said that. I did a feature on an over-40 soccer league. I don't even know the rules of the game."

"Irregardless, that gets your foot in the door, so to speak."

"Freddie, let's not do this right now. I'm sick of rehashing this. Look, I'm at the house, so I gotta go."

"Call me later," he said. "Gidget is dying to hook up with you!"

I was doubtful of that, or the great job Freddie had lined up for me, which would probably turn out to be clerking for the sports editor. No, I needed a clean break from everything. Maybe I should go south and stay with Dad awhile, find a gig with a beach view.

Holly Baird's house was on a shady street in Bryn Mawr, a trendy enclave not far from downtown Minneapolis. Not surprisingly, there was no answer when I rang the doorbell. I tried the number again, heard a phone ringing inside, but no one picked up. Walking around to the back of the house, I entered the alley. The garage door was closed. A forlorn metal patio table with a tattered green umbrella and one chair sat in the small back yard.

"She's not home," a voice called from the yard next door. A woman was pruning rose bushes along the low wooden fence separating the properties.

"Do you know where Holly is?" I asked.

"They left this morning," she said. "You a relative?"

"I work with her. She was supposed to work today and didn't show up."

"Oh. Well, she went out of town," the woman said. "I'm picking up the mail for them while they're gone."

"They?"

"Holly and Steve. Her husband."

"Did she say where they were going?"

"No, just that they would be out of town for a while."

"OK. Well, if you hear from her, could you tell her to call me?" I gave the woman my card. "It's pretty important."

She looked at the card and shrugged. "Sure. OK."

Again a dead end. Every which way I turned lately I ran into one of those. It was getting tiresome.

AFTER FINALLY LOCATING a parking spot in a packed lot near the convention center, I strode into the job fair brimming with confidence—a confidence that I was desperate to find something, anything, that would afford me a living wage far from my previous and current places of employ.

The aisles were jammed with people in similar situations, lost souls looking for a lifeline. The booths I passed were not in the least enticing—Navy recruiting, insurance sales, graduate school of business, culinary academy, big rig driving school. It seemed hopeless until I spotted a small stand in a corner of the cavernous room manned—or should I say womanned—by a young grunge.

"Hi, my name is Jim. Tell me about your music course."

"Hi, Jim. My name is Leslie," the young woman said. She had on a red plaid shirt over hole-y jeans, large black glasses and long black hair streaked with blue. In another life, we might have hung out together.

"What we offer is a three-month intensive course in music production. Not much theory but plenty of practical experience in the audio sphere. Do you play?"

"Uh, no, but I'm a great fan of music. I have this collection..."

"We're looking for serious candidates who want to further their progression into studio work. Is that what you're looking for?" she asked.

"Not really. I'm more of a music appreciation and archiving type," I explained. "Maybe something along the lines of a library of music or record-keeping."

"Record-keeping," she laughed. "Very good."

"No, I meant that—"

"You probably won't find a career in that," she said.

"Probably not."

"But there are studios across the country. Across the world, really, and they all need producers and engineers who have a keen eye—and ear—for mixing and perfecting the next big sound. Are you up to that challenge? Think about it." She handed me her card with the name of the company: Master Mixers of America.

Mixers sounded appealing but not the kind she had in mind. I headed out to find a bar.

43

While quenching my sudden thirst, Tina phoned in search of my whereabouts. "Not at the store currently," I replied. The less she knew the better.

"Well, you might want to get back here before the place blows up. Foster just shut down the maintenance department, and my union captain is pushing for a walkout. Just thought you'd like to know."

"Is something wrong in maintenance? Is there a gas leak or something?"

"No, and it's not temporary, either."

I had been saying this a lot lately, but in this situation, it was entirely appropriate: "What the hell?"

Tina offered no further opinion on what was going on, so I aimed my vehicle toward Hennepin. As I was turning into the parking facility, I caught a glimpse of someone that almost caused me to run into a concrete pillar. It was Emmie! After slamming on the brakes and narrowly averting a fender crunch, I looked back to see if it was really her, but she had already entered a stairwell.

My heart was pounding on the ride up to the ninth floor. Maybe she had come to her senses and was back at her post! Perhaps life would go on and I wouldn't have to leave the store! At least some small sliver of my existence could return to sanity!

Of course, my hopes were dashed when I saw that her desk was still vacant, and she was nowhere to be found in the executive suite.

To top it off, Detective Farraday was in the inner sanctum, waiting for me.

"Mr. Biersovich, can you tell me your whereabouts Monday afternoon?"

I had to think before answering. "I was at the store until around 1, then I went home for awhile. When I got the call about the body—"

"When was that? And who called you?"

"Joe T called me. Joseph Terrazzo, assistant to Mr. Scalabrino." Farraday was writing notes in a pad a bit smaller than mine. "It was late afternoon. I came in for awhile, but they didn't need my help anymore so I went home."

Farraday asked whether I had anyone who could corroborate my story. Freddie was my alibi for the time not at the store, but I wasn't sure bringing him into the equation was the right move. Farraday left with a suspicious look aimed at me.

I figured I had better warn Joe T that Farraday was on the warpath.

"Don't worry about me," he said when I phoned. "I can handle Iceland Yard."

"Beg pardon? What's Iceland Yard?"

"It's what those jokes of a detective bureau call themselves. You never heard that?"

"No, can't say that I have."

"What have you found out from the other clerks?"

"Nothing, really." I related the conversation with Britnie's co-workers and the disappearance of the friend who worked in bedding. "She went out of town with her husband. No idea where."

"She got scared off," Joe T said. "So we still have a threat inside the store."

"You think it's an employee of La Scala?"

"All indications point that way. Maybe this Holly shot the woman and then lammed. Find out what you can about her."

Sorry, I thought, Holly can wait. There's a higher priority mission on my plate. When I found Tina on the first floor she was sitting on a stool in a corner of the cosmetics counter. The crowd had dissipated and she looked beat.

"Have you seen Emmie?" I asked.

"Nice to see you too, Beers," she replied.

"Sorry. How's your day going?"

"I'm exhausted. I've had a line of grotesque ladies to paint from the opening gun, and it has finally slowed down. I think my hands are cramping. I'm calling in sick next time they do one of these sales."

"Has Emmie passed by here? I thought I saw her as I was pulling into the parking ramp."

"No, is she back?"

"Not sure. If it wasn't her, it was her doppelganger."

"Have you spoken with her?"

I shook my head and grimaced, recalling my last phone message.

"So what's this about maintenance?"

"Just what I told you. Foster shut them down."

"But how is that possible?"

"I don't know! Go see for yourself!"

I did just that. Instead of the usual blare of heavy metal coming from Bradley's boom box, the only sound was the opening and closing of file cabinet drawers. Don Anderson was in his office, packing boxes on his desk.

"What's going on, Don?"

"You tell me. We're closing up shop."

"But why?"

"Go ask Salmon Foster. He's the idiot that made this decision."

"But who's going to do maintenance?" I ran through the chores I had seen Anderson's department handle in the past, ranging from the simple, replacing light bulbs, to the more complex—replacing locks, supervising contract renovators and painters, and tuning up the heating and cooling systems.

He smirked. "Not my problem anymore. I'm retiring." He resumed packing the boxes with files and memorabilia.

"But what—"

"I told you, don't ask me. Foster." He pointed toward the ceiling.

As I rode back up to the ninth floor, the possible explanations swam through my cranium. Could this all be part of the same scheme Foster hatched in an attempt to remove Jane? Was he sabotaging the store? Or did the order come from higher up?

My notepad was filling up fast with questions, none of which I could answer.

44

Orders from Scalabrino," Foster said when I inquired about maintenance.

"That doesn't make sense," I replied.

"Irregardless."

"And why did you want to replace Jane Mertin?"

"We're finished here," he said dismissively. "Make sure you fill in Maria before you leave the store." He swiveled to gaze onto Hennepin, my cue that my presence was no longer wanted.

Somehow, I believed the answer to my questions was tied up with all that had transpired in the store since that fateful day of 9/11. Untangling the case of the La Scala murders wasn't my problem anymore, though. Farraday and his ilk could handle that. After all, that was their real job, whereas I had no business being in the business of detecting.

When I returned to my office, Maria and Vi weren't around. But Maria had left a note inviting me to a late lunch at a pub near the parkway. That might be good. Then I could swing by Scalabrino's digs and find out the real story behind the shutdown of maintenance.

Killing time, I wandered through the store. Still no sign of a clerk in bedding, but someone had thoughtfully left a sign on the counter: SLEEPING IT OFF—BACK LATER. Very funny.

On five, I found a former employee of the maintenance department, Bradley. He was mostly standing around observing while other clerks were busy selling watches.

I pulled him aside and asked what was going on.

"Bro, you tell me. All I know is they shut us down. No warning. Now I gotta learn about Rolexes and junk like that! What the fripp!"

"Don says he's retiring."

"Yeah! That's messed up, man! He said he was gonna promote me to assistant superintendent, and then I'd take his place when he retired. I'm screwed, dude!"

I couldn't picture slacker Bradley running a department, even if it was only maintenance. La Scala would likely fall apart under his watch. But I told him I would try to get to the bottom of it and warned him that being a watch salesman was a bit more demanding than his old job.

THE "GENUINE" English pub had the affectations of British culture without the true ambience. Maria was waiting for me in a booth, already halfway through a glass of beer. When the waiter came over, I ordered a Tadcaster, probably the only true artifact of the island in the place.

Vi had been telling Maria how great the pubs in London are, and she had been wanting to experience that. I looked around at the clientele and determined that the concept lost something in the translation.

She insisted on ordering bangers and mash, over my objection. I stuck with fish 'n' chips, a dish not likely to be so disappointing. Maria hadn't been to London, so she didn't know any better.

"You have anything you need to fill me in on before you depart our company?" Maria asked.

After a moment to consider, I answered no. "You've probably learned more from Jane's files in the last few days than I knew for the past few years. I had no clue about what she did. My role was limited to a small segment of the La Scala enterprise."

"You're too modest."

"No, just realistic. I addressed irate customers, an occasional shoplifter, served as liaison to the First Sentinel guards, walked around with the fire marshal."

"And security cameras? Jason Barth wants to review the contract for the installation."

"Well, that, yeah. Other than the special assignments, I didn't really do much."

"Special assignments?"

"Mr. Scalabrino had me look into certain...events."

"You went to Las Vegas."

"The whole Vegas thing. And I went to London to look at a possible store location, but that turned into a fiasco. And we had that other event," I said.

"Other event?"

"You didn't hear about the head in a box?"

"Oh, right. I did hear something about that. You'll have to tell me all the gory details," she said.

"Gory is right. Anyway, I think you're set. Are you staying here permanently?"

"Oh heavens, no! Minneapolis is too...small town for me. I need to be where the action is!"

There's action here, I thought, just not the kind I want to be around anymore. As I predicted, Maria's dish was less than satisfying. I shared some of my fish with her. She insisted she was going to take me out for a proper sendoff at the end of the week.

BACK AT THE STORE it was end-of-day business as usual. The early frenzy had died down to a normal flow of customers. Outside in the street, it was also the normal buzz of activity—four crewmen standing around talking while one actually did work in the pit. I figured that was the expected ratio of government industriousness—4:1 slackers to worker bees.

A tickle in the back of my head told me it might be a good idea to apply for a civil service position.

45

Wednesday, September 26

Just make it through the next 24 hours, I told myself as I ascended to the ninth floor. Unfortunately, that 24 hours was spread over three workdays I would have to endure before finally getting a taste of freedom.

I had passed beyond the trepidation of unemployment phase to the joy of leaving stage. I could imagine all my store co-workers smiling and sending me off with good wishes as I walked out at the end of the day Friday. Envision it and make it happen.

Until then, I was dealing with the dismal reality of La Scala drudgery. The rain started early and came down in buckets. No work commenced outside the store, which remained a scene of devastation. It seemed the street project was getting nowhere fast, just like my work life and love life.

I had decided that I could do nothing more in my remaining time at the store. Any further investigation into the murders would have to be the job of Farraday and his gang, despite what Joe T wanted me to do. There was little I could accomplish in three days time.

Freddie got hold of me early to invite me to go to the Vikings game with him on Sunday. They were hosting Tampa Bay at the Metrodome, hoping to get in the win column for the first time that season. I said why the hell not. He had a press box guest pass. I could suck up some freebies far above the rabble.

I'm not sure what drew me to the basement that morning. Perhaps morbid curiosity. No, I wasn't hoping to find another body. But I was befuddled about the demise of the maintenance

155

department. Perhaps Anderson was down there and could shed some light.

But he wasn't. Instead, there was a construction crew disassembling walls. Workmen had set up barricades at the periphery of the adjacent sporting goods department, but they were insufficient to keep out the din.

The nearest clerk couldn't provide any information, but he pointed me in the direction of the relatively new head of the section. His nametag said Connor.

"Can you tell me what's going on over there?" I asked him.

Connor looked nervous. "I'm afraid I can't. Mr. Foster wants to keep it quiet."

"I work with Salmon," I said. "Jim Biersovich, head of security. I've been out of the store and missed the briefing."

He considered for a second before spilling it. "They're expanding sporting goods," Connor said. "Adding exercise equipment. Apparently, orders of Mr. Scalabrino."

Ah, that made sense. Boss is on a new health kick. Sees opportunity for additional revenue stream, selling overpriced gear to stumpy, middle-aged folk. But that didn't explain what was going on with maintenance. I decided to skip Foster and go straight to the boss, since we were on a first-name basis.

"No, you can't speak to Johnny right now," Joe T told me when I rang the mansion.

"But I just want to ask him why—"

"He's not even here. He's taking his wife to the airport for her return to London."

That was a surprise. I thought maybe she would stick around. Was Scalabrino hoping to keep her in the States with an attempt to improve his physique? It didn't work, then.

"I just want to know why he shut down maintenance. Of all the departments to eliminate—"

"Why do you even care?" Joe T asked. "You're a short-timer. You don't care about the store anyway."

His words stung. More so because they were the truth. There really wasn't anything to care about anymore. Certainly not the job. And my love life was shot. Again. Even Dad had moved away, not to mention Lena. What was there left to keep me around?

THE CALL caught me by surprise. It was from Jane's younger son, Lex. He had finished going through his mother's house and cleaning it out for the real estate company. He had come across something he thought I might want to have.

Lacking any desire to hang around the store and pretend to work, I agreed to meet him at the house. It was an unassuming bungalow nestled amid tall trees in St. Louis Park. Lex showed me into the mostly cleared space, which would soon be staged for an open house.

"Last time we talked you mentioned something about some emails," I said.

"Oh, right. I printed them out for the cops. They said they would look into it," Lex said.

"Do you remember what the messages said?"

"Something about she wasn't the boss of the team. I assumed he was talking about the soccer team."

"He? Was there a name."

"Not really. I just assumed it was a guy because it was pretty mean. It said something to the effect of 'next time you try to boss me around I'll kick your ass.' "

"Wonder what that was about," I said. "Could be a work team. Maybe it was from someone on the management team. You remember the email address?"

"No, it was just a series of numbers and letters, like abc12345 at msn dot com. The cops were going to try to track it down, but they didn't think there was much chance of attaching it to a person."

It seemed like a vital piece of information that could lead to the identity of the killer. Or at least someone who held a grudge against Jane for some reason. Good thing it was in the hands of the police and not me. I wouldn't know where to begin to try to trace something in the cyber world. If Lena were here, she might. But again, out of my hands.

"So this thing I wanted you to see...it's this way." Lex led me through the dining room to the kitchen, which was still in the process of being cleaned out. Lex pointed to a picture on a wall in the breakfast nook.

"I didn't know if maybe you wanted to have it," he said.

The simple chrome frame contained a clipping of my story on Jane's over-40 soccer team, the assignment that triggered my escape from journalism into the world of retail. The main photo was a picture of a smiling Jane holding a soccer ball on her right hip, with other team members in the background, left feet propped on top of balls.

"I appreciate it but I have a copy of the story," I told him.

"Well, I thought you might want this one because of what's written on the back," he said.

46

ive this to Jim B. when I'm gone.

G The handwritten note on the back of the framed story obviously was intended for me, unless there was some other Jim B. in Jane's life. But seeing as I wrote the story and my byline was on it, it was logical to assume it was for me.

"I guess she wanted you to have it," Lex said.

"Thanks," I said, taking the offering. I wasn't sure what I would do with it. Unlikely I would hang it in my kitchen or anywhere else. I had whole scrapbooks of clipped stories serving as testament to my days in the rag trade. This one held no special place of importance, other than as a springboard to different employment, which I was now also abandoning.

The phrasing seemed odd. Was she anticipating something happening to her?

Lex inquired about Dad and what his plans were, so I filled him in. They had met once and Lex thought he was a nice guy, although for him, like me, it seemed weird to have a parent dating. Of course, that was all over now.

He had little information to offer on the whereabouts of his father, Jane's ex-husband. "He didn't come to the funeral and hasn't responded to my calls," Lex said.

"Was there animosity between your parents?"

Lex pondered for a moment. "I was 12 when they split. I remember lots of shouting, but I really wasn't paying much attention. Then suddenly Dad was gone. Mom didn't talk about it very much."

"What does your brother say?"

"We don't keep in touch very often," Lex said. "Charlie has had a bit of a...some problems."

"Like what? Health problems?"

"No, more like...legal problems. I really don't want to talk about it." Lex clammed up, so I didn't press the issue. But the continuing absence of her ex and older son put them squarely in the suspect category in my mind.

On the way back to work, I was held up by a huge traffic jam as I entered downtown. It took about 20 minutes to go two blocks. When I finally got to my parking spot, my nerves were shot. The hassle of fighting the construction backup on top of everything else further convinced me I was on the right course with my exit strategy.

"WHAT ARE YOU DOING Friday afternoon?"

The question caught me by surprise, not only because I had no plans but also because that had been the traditional time when Emmie and I celebrated the end of the work week with dinner and a movie or dinner and a concert or dinner and a quiet evening alone listening to my music.

For the past couple of weeks, there had been no plans because there had been no Emmie. This saddened me, but the new reality of my life dictated that I had to move out and move on.

Maria was waiting for an answer, so I told her I had no plans.

"Good," she said. "You're coming with me." She didn't elaborate and I didn't push her to elaborate. Although there was no future in our relationship, casual as it was, some brain cell deep in the recesses of my skull held a spark of hope that this would get me back on the romantic bandwagon.

Maria and Vi had gone through Jane's filing cabinets, found pertinent contracts and correspondence, and organized a binder of important papers to pass on to the next vice president of facilities, should there be one. Stacks of manila folders remained on just about every horizontal surface, however, and Maria asked for my help in returning them to the cabinets.

Without a real assignment for my final days, I assumed the role of filing clerk. Once that was accomplished, Maria had nothing more for me to do, so I wandered off, finding myself standing before the security video closet. I went in and stared at the monitors for a while, observing that commerce proceeded as normal.

I noted that Tina was busy as usual at the cosmetics counter and even Bradley was getting into the swing of things in watches. When the view switched to the basement, I saw that the reshaping of the former maintenance department was quickly progressing. It hardly looked like the same place.

In the space of a couple of weeks, everything had changed. One tragic day in September 2001 had altered the course of history, both mine personally and mankind's in general. Things would never be the same, I was convinced.

But as the great Yogi Berra once said, when you come to a fork in the road, take it. What else could I do?

A call woke me from my contemplative state. Joe T wanted me to drop everything—easy enough—and come out to the mansion for a chat. Why not, I thought. Wasn't doing anything productive. Maybe one last visit to the Scalabrino spread before I said goodbye. It was something to do.

SCALABRINO WAS in his suit behind his desk, the ubiquitous putter leaning against it to one side.

"Have a seat, Mr. Biersovich," he said, nodding to Joe T. "The usual?"

"Sure," I replied, not knowing which usual Joe T intended to prepare.

"I'll cut to the chase," Scalabrino said. "You have one more day in my employ. Then you're leaving us for a new...adventure."

I nodded. It was actually two more days but who was counting? Joe T handed me a short glass containing a clear, fizzy drink with a wedge of lime on the rim. A sip confirmed it was a G&T.

Scalabrino smiled. "I hate to see you go, but I understand, Mr. Biersovich...Jim."

"Thank you, Johnny."

"There's just one more thing I need you to do before you depart." Uh-oh, here it comes. "You may do this tomorrow at your leisure. I trust Maria has the official duties in hand."

"I think so."

"Very well. Then here's what I want you to do..."

THAT NIGHT I had a frightening glimpse into my future. I dreamed I had taken a job with Metro Transit but instead of driving a bus, I was picking up passengers on a bike.

It seemed like a great job—being outdoors, getting exercise, meeting people—until a tour group showed up at one stop. I was trying to figure out how to fit a dozen people on my 10-speed when I woke up, thankful that this was one career path I could cross off the list.

47

Thursday, September 27

The penultimate day of my employ at La Scala started with a bang. When I heard a heated argument coming from the direction of Salmon Foster's office, I knew something wicked had this way come.

No work was getting done in the executive suite as all personnel had halted to try to hear what the scrap was about. The door to Foster's office was closed, however, and his secretary, Candace, only offered that it was Jane Mertin's ex-husband providing the noise.

Soon, a First Sentinel guard arrived and escorted the man from the premises. He was a regular-looking guy dressed in what appeared to be medical scrubs of a sort of greenish tint. I tried to remember any details about him from conversations with Jane, but nothing came to mind.

A bit later Candace filled me in. The ex had demanded release of all Jane's office possessions to him, a proposition Foster balked at, probably because he doesn't like taking orders from anyone.

Besides, there was precious little in Jane's office of a personal nature, just a couple of photos of her sons and one of her soccer squad, plus the sort of innocuous knickknacks that adorn any workstation: a snow globe of Grenoble, a drinking bird toy from Wiesbaden, a pewter ashtray marked "Made on Pluto" and a few other items. Why anyone would want that stuff was beyond me, although I could understand a parent wanting photos of his offspring.

Candace also inquired about what sort of cake I would like for the party on my last day.

"No cake is the sort I would like," I replied.

"No cake? But everyone has cake on the last day," she said. "It's a tradition up here on the ninth floor."

"I just want my departure to be low-key," I explained. "It's not like I'm retiring after a 30-year career. I've only been here a couple of years."

Candace looked crestfallen. The cake was just as much for the people who were staying as it was for me—maybe more—and I was depriving them of that.

"OK, perhaps a small cake," I relented. "But no big production, OK? Most of the people up here don't even know who I am anyway."

She smiled. "Beers, everyone knows you! And we hate to see you go." She gave my arm a squeeze and headed back to her desk.

I figured a little cake wouldn't hurt. Let them eat cake, I thought, then I remembered that the person who uttered that phrase, Marie Antoinette, had soon after lost her head.

WHILE CONTEMPLATING how to attend to Scalabrino's "secret mission," I again fell into rumination about my fuzzy future. I attempted to picture myself in various career settings, but nothing seemed to ring true.

A number of songs wafted through my gray matter, finally settling into a groove by Nilsson, "The Lottery Song": *Life is just a gamble, gamble if you want to win.* After a while, I took the song's advice, fished the card out of my wallet and *let the wheel of fortune spin.*

Leslie was glad I called. She was expecting me to, she said, because she saw a hunger in me that she didn't see in many applicants to the music production course. In fact, it was fortuitous that I called, she said, because there was a field trip planned for prospective students that weekend if I wanted to attend. I said sure, why not.

WHEN FREDDIE CALLED, I determined he would not get into my head and mess up my day. After all, I was a short-timer, counting down the hours to freedom.

As usual, I was wrong, and Freddie quickly turned my mood.

"I've been thinking..." he began. Groan. Always a bad omen.

"What is it, Freddie? Kinda busy here trying to cross all the I's and dot all the T's before I leave."

"Do you ever wonder why we drive on the right side of the road, but the steering wheel is on the left? I mean, when we were in England, it was the opposite. So maybe we're doing it wrong."

"I don't know, Freddie."

"Or maybe the steering wheel should be in the middle. Did you ever think of that?"

"It's probably on the left so you can see oncoming traffic and stay in your lane without having a head-on collision."

"I was at a Twins game the other day and got to wondering why the pitcher stands on a little hill but nobody else does. Seems a bit unfair."

"Freddie, I really don't have time for this..."

"Football should really be called handball. Seventy-five percent of the time they're passing or handing off the ball. Of course, there's already a game called handball..."

"You do realize that—"

"And what about paint? Some guy on TV was talking about how paint isn't really the color you think it is. It's just a trick of light reflection that makes your eyes think it's a color. That's why color-blind people see different colors—because they've got something broken in their light receptors."

Sigh. This could go on forever, I thought. When Freddie got into one of his philosophical moods, the stream of consciousness—or more likely puddle of consciousness—could be bizarre and never-ending.

"Gotta go," I said, and abruptly hung up. It was a mean thing to do, but my befuddled brain needed no more clouding of the Freddie variety.

48

Without a valid reason to stall, I headed down to the basement to complete Scalabrino's final request. I found the guy right away, standing in the middle of his new realm, supervising the placement of exercise equipment.

He looked to be in his 30s, a bit taller than me, with short blond hair and wearing a La Scala branded warmup suit.

"Dean? Hi, I'm Jim Biersovich."

"How are you, Jim?" He grasped my hand with a bodybuilder's grip.

"Mr. Scalabrino asked me to come down and see if there's anything you need, if the space is sufficient and so on."

"No, it's great," he said. "Can't wait to get started. We're doing a soft opening this weekend, but the big splash is for Monday. I think they're doing some promo spots with one of our employees."

Probably Bambi, I thought. She seemed to have a way to get the bodies in the store.

As I glanced around the space, I had difficulty remembering the layout of the former maintenance department. The walls had been removed and it looked like an entirely new area, bright, clean and vibrant. Certainly more enticing than the grungy maintenance dungeon.

"Cool. Well, I'm head of security." A title I would have for another 24 hours or so, I thought. "Johnny wanted to make sure you had whatever you needed to protect the equipment." The place was full of very expensive looking gear.

"I think we're set, man. Nobody's gonna walk out with one of these babies," he said, slapping his hand on a nearby treadmill. "And as far as safety, we have two instructors slash sales associates starting Saturday, so they can make sure no one gets hurt." He gave me a broad smile.

"That's great." He walked me through the department, pointing out the features of each apparatus, ranging from simple one-function machines, like the treadmills, to multi-faceted full-body-workout devices.

"So you came from another store?" I inquired.

"No, I've never been a salesman," he replied. "I worked for Parks and Recreation up in Shoreview. Did some exercise classes and ran some of the adult leagues. Fun job, but I was ready to try something new."

One of the team assembling the displays asked Dean about placement of the speakers. He pointed to a spot in the far corner.

"Speakers?" I asked.

"We're putting in a sound system," he explained. "Gotta have a little music to ramp up the energy. That's what we're all about!"

He seemed a little too enthusiastic for La Scala but maybe the store could use an injection of adrenalin.

Eager to complete my final assignment for the boss, I gave Joe T a call to report. It was the old Columbo routine—just one more thing. I had no choice but to indulge him as I wound down the clock to early retirement, or "phase three," as Freddie would call it.

IN THE MIDDLE of completing my absolutely last task at Jane's old desk, Freddie called again. He delivered his expected offer of easing my path back to journalism, minus the philosophical musings, which I routinely declined. Then he demanded that I go out with him after work, which I accepted.

I was just finishing up the last of my report and getting ready to hit print when a girl from personnel popped her head in the office and said there was someone asking about me. When I followed her down the corridor and entered personnel, my heart went into pound mode. Emmie was there, sitting in a chair.

Thousands of thoughts, all jumbled together, raced through my head. Was she back? Had she finally come to her senses and returned to work? Was I leaving right when she was returning? What was in the box on the floor next to her chair?

"Emmie, I'm so glad—"

"Hello, Jim," she said. "I just came back to get some things." She waved a hand toward the box.

"Wait, what? You're not—"

"I have officially resigned," she said quietly. "I'm moving back in with my folks. I can't be here anymore."

"But but but—" My babbling tongue and addled brain were out of sync and unable to coordinate to produce a coherent thought.

"It's not you," she added, then smiled. "I enjoyed our time together. You're a great guy, Jim."

Well, that was some consolation. Very little, actually.

"Emmie, don't do this."

"I have to," she replied. One of the girls from personnel then approached Emmie and handed her an envelope, presumably her final paycheck. Emmie took it and stood to go.

"Can we just go get a cup of coffee or something?" I asked.

She smiled again. "I have to go. My mother is waiting for me in the car."

"Emmie, don't leave," I pleaded. "I...I love you." This declaration stunned me, along with several of the personnel staff in close proximity. But Emmie seemed unmoved.

"I know. I feel the same about you, Jim. But this is the way it has to be. I can't stay in the Twin Cities."

"But why? I don't understand."

Emmie picked up the box and nodded for me to follow her. She stopped when we got to the elevator.

"Every day, I wake to the vision of Jane..." She didn't finish the sentence. "It doesn't leave me. Just being in this building, where it happened, horrifies me. It's not something I can forget and just carry on like everything is OK." She smiled. "It's not OK. But it's better when I'm far away from here."

"Emmie, I want to be with you," I said. "I'm quitting my job here. Tomorrow is my last day. I don't know what's next. Anything is possible. I could move to Indianapolis and find a job there. I just want—"

"No, Jim," she said, putting a hand to my cheek. "I'll always cherish our time together, but this place and everything that happened here has to be in my past. I have to move ahead. You are a reminder of..." She looked down, started crying, then punched the elevator button.

"I'm sorry" was the last thing she said as the doors closed and Emmie disappeared from my life.

49

Toward the end of the day, Tina came by with a gift.

"I'm gonna miss you, Beers," she said, handing me what was obviously an LP in La Scala silver paper. The quality of the bow told me this had been wrapped at the gift counter. I was shocked to discover an original pressing of The Left Banke's debut album, featuring the hit "Walk Away Renee."

"Tina, thank you! How did you...?"

"Guy at the used record shop told me it was rare, had just come in and he was reluctant to part with it. I had to pay over list."

"You shouldn't have—"

She hugged me before I could complete my sentence then walked away silently. The choked-up feeling that followed told me here was yet another reason why my departure from La Scala was so painful. Tina had become a good friend in the short time we had worked together. But she was tough and would be fine, I had no doubt. For myself, the jury was still out.

Maria was beaming behind Jane's desk when I returned to the office.

"You look happy," I commented.

"Had a small victory today," she replied. "Street crew just informed us they plan to finish up next week, so traffic can return to some semblance of sanity."

"That's good. What lit a fire under them?"

"Not sure. Johnny is coming in tomorrow for your last day."

"Really? Why?"

"He wants to get a look at the new fitness spa."

"Is that what they're calling it?"

"Sounds a little sexier than gym equipment," she said. "I may have to go down there and show him around. That new guy is kinda cute." She giggled.

"Dean? I don't think he's your type."

"Why? What's wrong with him?"

I couldn't respond to that. I had a vibe from the guy that signaled a creep alert. "Just be careful," I cautioned.

SAM WAS POPPING the cap on a Summit Oktoberfest for me as I entered The Crater. I spotted Freddie at a corner table.

"On the house," Sam said, pushing the bottle toward me. "A sending-off present."

I thanked him and headed to the table. I knew what was coming as soon as the first words left Freddie's mouth: "Now hear me out." He went into a long spiel about my meager prospects outside the newspaper trade, the need to re-center my life and get back on a solid footing, the advantages of being around his magical aura as a chick magnet. I let him drone on without a reply.

We had drained our beers by the time he ran out of steam. Freddie graciously accepted my unspoken offer to buy a round. When it arrived, he said, "Well? What do you think? Convinced yet?"

I knew the only way to get him to stop hounding me about returning to my former life was to do exactly that. But there was no way on earth I was going to do that, even if I had to go on unemployment until I found a suitable job. Journalism just had no attraction for me anymore.

"Freddie, I'm going to tell you this one more time, and then we can drop it. You're just wasting your time and mine by continuing to harass me on this subject. It's not gonna happen. So just accept it. I'm not going back. Period. End of discussion."

"But—"

"NO!" I bellowed. Nearby patrons looked up at my outburst. I felt a bit abashed, but I was tired of this continual campaign by Freddie. It was far past time for his one-track brain to process the information and give up. He sighed and swigged his beer.

"You want to hit the movies with me tomorrow night? *2001* is playing in Eagan. Haven't seen that in years on the big screen. And I've got a girl you're going to want to meet."

A blind date? Seriously? That would be the last thing on my agenda. "I'm busy," I replied.

"So what are you gonna do on your last day to go out in style? Set off the fire alarm? Knock over some clothes racks?"

"Freddie, I'm leaving on good terms. Why would I want to do something that would put a black mark on my record?"

"Your record! Hah!"

I shook my head. Freddie just didn't get it. I sometimes wondered why we were friends at all. We didn't have much in common, other than having worked together for a couple of years. His thought processes were a universe removed from mine—or most of mankind, for that matter. If I made a total break and moved from the Twin Cities, I doubted I would have much contact with him at all.

In fact, the prospect of moving far away seemed to be growing at the back of my mind. There was very little to keep me rooted to that location. The weather sucked for half a year. Surviving bone-numbing cold and icy roads grew tiresome. Maybe it was time to get out before another winter caught me in its death grip.

As I was lost in contemplation, Freddie said, "That's the record you need to listen to." He threw his thumb back over his shoulder in the direction of the jukebox. Someone had selected "Time" by Pink Floyd, a song about the incessant clock on one's lifespan, a tune whose depressing lyrics were offset by one of the most memorable melodies in rock history.

It was a song that I had listened to countless times, immersed in the sounds of perhaps the greatest album of the prog rock era. I had heard it and understood the meaning, or so I thought. Now it had even more significance in my life.

For certain, no one had told me when to run, but I was definitely hearing the starting gun.

50

Friday, September 28

The final day of my employment at La Scala dawned without fanfare. I arose, drank coffee, showered and left for the office in the same manner as I had for the previous two and a half years.

It was real and surreal at the same time.

Tina glanced at me and turned away as I passed the cosmetics counter on the main floor. She appeared to be snubbing me, but I could understand she was hiding her pain. We had become friends, and it always hurts to see one leave your daily environment.

There was a package sitting on the desk when I entered Jane's office. A card affixed to it said: "From Vi and Maria." It was small and square, a bit larger than a box for a baseball. I imagined a ball signed by the Twins or maybe a paperweight was inside, but I didn't have the heart to open it.

Somehow an hour slipped past, and I was still sitting in the office, doing lots of nothing. This is ridiculous, I thought. So I got up and determined I would make my final rounds of the store, starting in the basement.

In contrast to the normally staid demeanor of the rest of the building, the fitness department was jumping, literally. A leotard-clad young woman was demonstrating an aerobics routine for a small group of customers, most of them pudgy. A driving rock tune was propelling her momentum. Large screens on the back wall displayed a strongman competition and a kickboxing match, delivering a not-so-subtle message to viewers: Get up and work your body! After purchasing our exercise equipment, of course.

All that activity was making me tired, so I fled to the first floor. Business was slow at the cosmetics counter, and Tina wasn't around at the moment. Plenty of patrons were shopping in sportswear, however, perhaps heeding the call to be wild one floor below.

Commerce was more routine on the third and fourth floors, where women were poring over the latest footwear and intimate garments. On five, it was a young crowd milling through electronics, looking for the latest device to make their lives livelier.

Depression set in on the fifth floor as I passed the jewelry counter. I still wasn't used to the absence of Lena, whose big and brash demeanor lured customers like a siren call. It was an affirmation that I was on the right track, the exit lane. La Scala just wasn't the same without Lena.

Bradley was standing around, staring into space at the watch counter, so I went over to say hi.

"Dude, you need to see something on the tapes," he said.

"What are you talking about?" I asked.

"The tapes?" He pointed to the camera aimed at his area. "I've got a break at 11:30 for lunch if you want to see it."

"Can you just tell me what it is?"

"No can do, kemo sabe. You just need to see for yourself."

"Another thief?" Bradley shook his head. "OK, whatever."

Knowing Bradley as I did, it was probably just a shot of a buxom patron's cleavage. But I would humor him since I really had nothing better to do.

Only once on my excursion through the building was I asked to perform my official duties. I was in the break room on seven, getting a soft drink, when a clerk I recognized from kitchenware lit into me.

"You need to do something about the thievery RIGHT NOW!" she said, invading my personal space.

"I'm sorry. Carmen, is it? Was there a shoplifter?"

"No, nothing like that," she said, inching even closer. "The thief that keeps stealing my pudding from the fridge." She pointed to the ancient pistachio green appliance in the corner, an item I had refused to explore for fear of contracting a mold disease.

"I don't know anything about—"

"You need to kick their ass!" she shouted, inches from my face. I was afraid she was going to do just that to me if I didn't get on her case pronto. So I promised I would put it as a top priority and skedaddled back up to nine before Carmen the space invader got physical.

There was a note stuck to the door of Jane's office when I returned. "Exit interview – 1 PM – Conference Room." I wasn't sure whose handwriting it was but probably Foster's secretary, Candace. Why I needed an exit interview escaped me, but I would humor whoever.

As I was collecting artifacts from my filing cabinet—cassettes, old notepads and various La Scala swag—Maria showed up.

"Did you like it?" she asked.

"Like what?"

"The gift, dummy! That looked like something you could use," she replied.

"Oh, no. I haven't opened it yet," I said, a bit embarrassed. "Busy."

Maria grabbed the box from the corner of the desk and shoved it into my hands. "You'll never guess." She sat and waited.

"Should I guess?" I asked, stalling. I really wanted to slink out quietly without a lot of fanfare and showering with gifts. Fade into the sunset—that was my style.

"Just open it," she said.

I did. The box revealed a plastic and glass device a bit larger than a pack of cards. On the front at the bottom was a wheel with a button in the middle. Above that was a blank piece of glass. Next to the item was a white cord that split to end at a pair of small knobs.

"Gee...thanks?" I said.

"Beers, you're holding the future in your hands," Maria beamed.

"OK? What is it?"

"That, my friend, is called an iPod."

I looked back down at the device, still clueless as to what it was. She proceeded to explain that it was a new piece of technology that would allow me to carry around hundreds of tunes and access them immediately, like a portable jukebox. Apple produced it and was about to release it to the public. This was a prototype sent to her by a friend at the company.

Maria assured me it was going to revolutionize music as we knew it. I was skeptical, naturally, but thanked her for thinking of me. I wasn't certain about its lasting appeal, but I told her I would look at it when I had time on my hands.

She reminded me to be ready for the big party after lunch, and cocktails following my last hour at La Scala. I told her I didn't want a big party, but cocktails sounded great.

AT MIDMORNING, while I was going through my filing cabinet, Maria was summoned to Foster's office, leaving me to pack up in private. Most of the contents of my files were expendable and wound up in the trash. I filled Jane's can and had just about filled the one at Emmie's old desk when Maria returned.

"Holy shit," she exclaimed. "This place is way more fucked up than Las Vegas."

"What's going on?" I asked.

"Did you see the paper?" I shook my head and she quickly departed. In a minute she was back and thrust a copy of the day's editorial page at me. On it was a letter from a reader named Clive Remson, laying out the arguments for a shutdown of La Scala, permanently. He claimed there was precedent for government to refuse to renew occupational permits due to the ongoing problems, even suggesting heavy fines for violation of state and local laws. By the time I got to the end of the lengthy letter, I sensed myself getting very angry.

"Who the hell is Clive Remson?" I asked.

"Foster thinks it's a pseudonym for Clete Ronson. He's a former city councilman and also the attorney for Brand X."

"I don't know who that—oh, you mean the enemy store."

"Exactly. So Foster is going on the offensive. He sicced Farraday on them, dropped lots of hints about political motivation regarding the street project, the picketing, harassment by the paper..."

"That would explain a lot."

"And murder."

This statement stopped me dead in my tracks. "Murder? You think they're behind Jane's death?"

"And the clerk. All part of the assault on La Scala. Uncle Joe says it all fits."

"I don't know..."

"Anyway, the owner of that store has a lot of questions to answer."

This was a bizarre development, but now that I thought about it, it made sense. La Scala had been doing well in recent years, according to the vague snippets of conversation I had overheard in the executive suite. And the rival concern had taken a hit in revenue.

Money was a great motivator, apparently.

51

Around 11:30 Bradley popped his head into the office and beckoned me down the back hall to the video surveillance room.

"Watch this," he said, inserting a tape into the slot under the desk. In seconds an image appeared on the screen in the lower right corner, where normally there's a view of the rear loading ramp. The scene was of the newly refurbished maintenance department, where rows of gleaming exercise machines were lined up.

Nothing happened for a couple of minutes, just customers walking past. Then a figure came into view. It was the back side of a man dressed in jeans and a long-sleeve khaki shirt. He stopped, glanced from side to side, then advanced on a treadmill. He knelt down and put an object under the treadmill before getting up and moving off. He kept his face away from the camera.

"What the hell did he do?" I asked.

"Put this under that machine," Bradley said, opening a drawer of the desk and pulling out an object. It was a deflated soccer ball. I looked it over but there wasn't anything out of the norm.

"Is it one of ours?" I asked.

Bradley shrugged.

"Who was he?"

"Dunno," Bradley said.

It was mysterious but seemed to be just another bizarre occurrence in retail land. Certainly nothing that I would have to contend with during my last few hours in captivity. I told Bradley to bring it to sporting goods and departed to resume my housecleaning.

At the back of the file cabinet was a folder with my hiring paperwork. There was a sheet on the dress code (which I regularly violated), information about health and retirement benefits, a copy of my job description and a clipping of the story I wrote on Jane's soccer team. It was the thing that convinced her I was an "earnest young man" looking for a new challenge.

Jane smiled at me from a lifetime removed in the photo. If only I could see her face again and have a proper farewell. I began reading:

These Rockettes Really Get Their Kicks

By Jim Biersovich

Herald sportswriter

Stumper is bent over on the sidelines, hands on knees, gasping for breath. "Coach...I need...a breather."

Beside her, Wingnut is sprawled on the ground, panting. The rest of the crew, hands on hips, observes from the field.

Coach is Jane Mertin, the leader of this ragtag bunch of women trying to enjoy a bit of recreation on a soccer field. It's an over-40 league, and this group is learning the hard way that it's a young person's game.

"We come out here for fun, to enjoy the sunshine and fresh air. And maybe get a little exercise in the bargain," Mertin explains.

They've only been at it for 20 minutes on this day. But the rigors of the game are pushing most of these players, out-of-shape office workers, beyond the brink of their endurance.

This is fun.

The league is composed of six teams that play on weekends at Shamrock Park in Shoreview. Each team has a sponsor. Mertin's squad is sponsored by Viking King Construction.

The team name is the Rockets but Mertin and others like to put the accent on the last syllable. "We're Rock*ettes* because we like to kick," she says.

After a water break, Stumper and Wingnut are ready for more. They are determined to get in shape, as are the rest of the ladies, because of an impending match with the

Screaming Meemies. Rumor has it that one of the opponent's players was on the Olympic squad in 1996. That seems a daunting prospect for the Rockets.

After all, we're talking about desk jockeys, not athletes. Among the group are two secretaries, a nurse, a department store executive, three housewives and

continued on Page D4

The story jumped, but that portion wasn't in the folder. I wracked my brain to remember the rest of the article, but that was a pointless exercise with my deficient memory. There was probably a copy of the full story in my apartment somewhere. But reading the whole thing wouldn't bring Jane back. Or Emmie, for that matter.

Maria walked in and announced, "They've moved your exit interview up. You're wanted in the conference room."

Might as well get it over with, I thought. However, if they were hoping for any scintillating revelations from me, they were in for a disappointment.

When I opened the door to the conference room, I was immediately confused. I expected there to be one other person in the room, most likely the head of human resources. But there was a crowd, every seat filled and more lining the walls.

Foster was there at the end of the table, along with most of the inhabitants of the executive suite. Bambi was stationed at a side table, standing behind a large sheet cake and wielding a long knife.

"You've arrived," a voice behind me said. "Let us begin." I turned to see Johnny Scalabrino in a velvet La Scala warmup suit, holding his putter against his shoulder.

The realization dawned on me: This was no exit interview. It was a cake sendoff.

"As you know, Mr. Biersovich has decided to part ways with our establishment," Scalabrino said. "I do not wish to see him go, but he is determined to continue his life adventure outside the confines of La Scala.

"You may or may not know that I have come to rely upon him heavily in the past two years. Mr. Biersovich...Jim...Beers to some of you..." There were giggles. "...has been instrumental behind the scenes in protecting this business from devastating circumstances. He is too modest to say that, so I am telling you now.

"We are currently in the midst of a crisis, with a number of challenges facing our store. I would like to have the expertise of...Beers...to tackle that for us all, but he has chosen a new path. We must all work diligently to protect our jobs as efficiently as he has in the past. I trust we will find a way. Maybe not the Beers way, but a way.

"Anyway, I wish you all the best, Jim. I have the utmost confidence that you will succeed admirably in whatever endeavor you undertake outside these walls."

Scalabrino began clapping and was quickly joined by everyone else in the room. When it died down, he said, "Perhaps you would like to say a few words, Jim?"

No, I wouldn't. I wasn't prepared for this. But I had to say something. After pondering a couple of options, I said simply: "Let's eat cake." Bambi took that as her cue and attacked the concoction, which was decorated with a La Scala logo and "Good Luck, Beers" in red icing.

During the course of the feast to follow, I shook hands with or was hugged by everyone in the room, including Scalabrino. Bambi gave me an embrace, and I marveled at the firmness and girth of her massive chest as it pressed against me.

Candace slipped me a $250 La Scala gift certificate and even Foster joined in, pressing a bottle of single malt scotch from his private stash into my hand.

By the time I finished my duties as a one-person receiving line, the cake had been consumed and only crumbs were left. Oh well, I thought. Let them drink scotch.

52

I resisted the temptation to crack open the bottle and sample the ocher liquid. I mean, it was my last day. What could they do—fire me? But I thought it best to save it for an after-work celebration.

Scalabrino popped his head in the office as I was finishing my packing, telling me he would uphold his end of the bargain. I should keep in touch with Joe T on my whereabouts.

With the last of my belongings boxed up, I turned my attention to the device sitting on top of the stack, Maria's gift. I plugged in the earphones and fiddled with it until music blared in my ears. I managed to turn it down to a less eardrum-shattering level.

Steely Dan was belting out "Reelin' in the Years," and I found myself bobbing my head to the tune. The next song was "Alive and Kicking" by Simple Minds, followed by George Harrison crooning "What Is Life."

I somehow switched off the device and conceded that Maria knew what she was talking about. Here was a medley of disparate artists assembled into an unlikely mini-jukebox. No telling what other songs were on the iPod. Perhaps I could discover them while consuming a glass of single malt that evening.

Then I got to thinking about the meaning of the numbers I had just heard. I was indeed reeling in years. Time was passing more rapidly, and I was impelled to move on. While I was "alive and kicking," Jane wasn't anymore, and that saddened me. And I wondered what my life would become without Emmie by my side.

As always, music spoke to me. There was a deeper meaning for me in almost every rock tune I heard. This was a hazard since so much of rock music was about loss, tragedy, unfulfilled hopes. I felt the singer's pain in every syllable.

What the hell. I opened the bottle and took a small swig, letting the warmth flow through my gullet. It was mighty smooth. I would certainly enjoy this later.

While I was toting boxes to my car, Freddie called.

"Beers, are you aware that you can freeze just about anything in the world? But there's one thing you can't freeze."

Normally, a Freddie conversation would drive me to the precipice and make me want to jump off. But today, with the weight of La Scala falling away, I was more copacetic and willing to engage my nutty friend in his insane ramblings.

"Time?" I asked.

"No, I'm talking food here. You can freeze potatoes and carrots and squash and broccoli, meat and fish, juice, soup, bananas, strawberries, blueberries, peaches..."

"Vodka won't freeze."

"I'm talking about things that if you freeze them, they're fine when they thaw out. Everything except this one thing."

"Human heads?"

"I'm being serious, Beers. It really bothers me that you can freeze everything in the universe but this one item."

"Why do you care?"

"Because if I figure out how to do it, I'll be a millionaire. No, a billionaire. I'll be living on easy street. You don't have any clue what I'm talking about, do you?"

"Do I ever, Freddie?"

"This is important. I need to know why this doesn't work. I want to invent a solution."

"OK. What is it?"

"Not gonna hazard a guess?"

"Let me sleep on it and I'll get back to you next week."

"It's lettuce. You can't freeze lettuce."

"OK."

"Aren't you going to ask how I know?"

"It's obvious. You froze some, pulled it out of the freezer expecting to use it and discovered that it had turned to mush."

"Not necessarily."

"Freddie, I know you. That's exactly what happened, correct?"

He was a little mortified and conceded it was.

"Help me figure this out, and I'll cut you in on the deal," he said.

"Sure, Freddie, just as soon as I solve that pesky world peace problem."

"Hey, when are you free of your chains?"

"Pretty soon."

"We need to go out and celebrate your return to your senses. We can start at The Crater and—"

"Got plans already, bud."

"Is it a—"

"Gotta go," I said, hanging up before the grilling.

NOW WHAT, I asked myself. The car was packed with my two small boxes of work junk, plus my Rolling Stones trash can. I should make another pass through, one last time, and tell everyone goodbye.

Or not.

Prolonging it just wasn't my style. Best to just leave quietly, become a part of La Scala's past, and let my co-workers get on with their business.

It was still early, so I had time to dump my boxes at the apartment before heading out for the evening's event. They really didn't have anything terribly compelling in them, so I just stacked them in the spare bedroom with the unsorted goods I had acquired at previous scavenger hunts for music.

There were four boxes of records, tapes, 8-tracks and assorted audio gear that hadn't made it into the collection proper. With the job a thing of the past, I would now have time to tackle those boxes.

The article on Jane had piqued my interest, so I decided to read the rest of the story. When I went to look for it, however, I couldn't find it. I had misplaced my clipping file or maybe lost it altogether. Had I inadvertently thrown it out with the recycling?

I could probably find it on microfilm at the library. Or even online, if I knew how to search. But a tear sheet would be nice to have. The framed story was good but incomplete.

Fortunately, I got Freddie's answering machine and was able to leave a succinct message asking him to acquire a back issue, for which he would be handsomely repaid.

Done and done, and now for some fun.

53

Maria was in an amazing mood. By amazing, I mean slightly tipsy. She apparently had had some pre-cocktails before our cocktail hour at the Grand Hotel, some posh digs for her temporary home.

She asked me if I wanted a drink either in the bar or in her room. Tempting. Very tempting. I took the high road, however, and suggested we visit the bar. While waiting for our drinks to arrive, she informed me that she had been offered a full-time position at the home store, which she outright declined.

"I told Uncle Joe I wouldn't survive here," she explained. "The climate, the whole vibe is so foreign to me." She laughed. "I don't know how you can stand it!"

"You get used to it," I said. "Well, maybe not the winters, unless you're from here."

"I'm from Virginia. We didn't have that kind of cold."

"What brought you to Las Vegas?" I asked.

Maria took a big gulp of her newly arrived martini and began, "It's a long story, but I'll condense it. I had a chance to get on with an aerospace company in the Northwest. They had a recruiting weekend at the Mirage. I just happened to be in town with a couple of girlfriends on a mini-vacation.

"I don't know why we decided to go to the recruiting session. Well, I know why. My friend Laura dared me. Plus I had a little liquid fortification—" She hoisted her martini glass. "Next thing I know I'm getting pushed to the front of the line and pulled into a room for grilling by some nerdy-looking types. Two of them were women.

"They apparently wanted to get more females into the workplace. They didn't care that I didn't have an engineering background. They just wanted sharp people who were quick learners. I must have impressed them, although I can't remember much of what I said in that room. Because they offered to fly me up to Spokane and tour the facility to see if it was something I wanted to do."

"Did you go?"

"No. I was tempted. I thought about it that evening and decided I would play the roulette wheel, let it decide my fate. Even, I went for it. Odd, I blew it off."

"And?"

"I don't even remember what it was, but I won $132 and was hooked. I looked around at the casino I was in—Bally's, I think—and decided that was more my kind of scene. Next day, I applied for a job."

"You worked at Bally's?"

"La Scala. Hey, gotta use whatever contacts you got, right? I just happened to know the owner, and Uncle Joe almost did a back flip when I expressed interest in going into the 'family business.' I said I would do it on one condition—I wasn't wearing any crappy uniform."

"You're pretty stylish for a blackjack dealer," I noted.

"Brings in the customers, so they don't complain. I usually have quite a few gamblers waiting for a chair. Put on a little floor show—that's what Las Vegas is all about." She smiled at me.

Couldn't argue with that. I also colored outside the lines at La Scala with my choice of attire, although I was in a lower-profile position than Maria.

After she finished her drink, she stood up, threw some bills on the table and said, "C'mon. I've got a bottle of cognac in the room with your name on it."

On the elevator ride up, I tried to gauge where the evening was heading. I had been in this situation before, even in Vegas, and calculated there was a 50 percent chance I would get an offer I couldn't refuse.

I was nervous and scrambled to make small talk. "That must be some bottle of cognac," I said. "A cognac called Beers." I grinned at Maria. She gave me a half-smile, took my hand and led me down the hallway to her room.

I just thought I had a luxurious room when I was in Las Vegas. That was a hovel compared to this. It was as big as a modest home, with a formal sitting room with big picture windows and a bar along one wall, full kitchen with island, a formal dining area and a door leading to what I suspected was a bedroom.

Maria got behind the bar and pulled out the cognac and two snifters, then poured. I took the one offered and sipped. She did likewise, then motioned me to join her on the couch.

"So now what?" she asked.

That was an open-ended question I didn't quite know how to answer. Now we have another drink? Now we make out? Or was she speaking about my future prospects? That could be answered: "Now what, indeed." I didn't get an opportunity to pick a valid response before she spoke again.

"So how do you like the iPod?"

"That thing is great," I said. "Really, I wasn't expecting it to be as nice as it is."

"You don't latch on to new technology very well, do you?"

Which was the understatement of the new millennium.

"No, I prefer some of the old stuff."

"Yet you have a cell phone."

"True."

"And you like the iPod."

"It's just so unusual. I mean, you put some really fine songs on there. I didn't expect I would get into it this quickly."

"You're welcome. Vi helped pick the songs." She finished off her drink and headed for the bedroom door. I contemplated whether she was just going to the bathroom or perhaps she was ready to call it a night. My answer came when she stopped in the doorway, turned around and said, "Well?"

A loaded question. From a semi-loaded woman. I put down my drink and followed her to the inner sanctum.

54

Saturday, September 29

Istumbled into my own bed in the wee hours but was too tired to sleep. I lay awake thinking about everything that had transpired, both that evening and in the preceding two weeks.

Had I made a mistake? Or many mistakes? Actually, had I done anything right?

There was a twinge of guilt, that I had cheated on Emmie. But that was edged out by the certainty that it's not cheating if the relationship is kaput.

Sleep was futile, so I got up, put on the coffee and determined to chart a path. A roadmap to my future. A direction and purpose.

I wound up staring at my wall of music, looking for the answer in a song. For once, I failed to feel the tug toward a particular ditty that might ease my malaise.

Hang on, Sloopy. Just as I was about to give up and return to my attempted slumbers, I remembered the iPod. I had discovered only a few of the tunes it concealed, so now was as good a time as ever to resume the exploration.

Songs ran the gamut from classic rock to classical, country, blues, disco and even rap. It was an eclectic mix, not all to my liking. Perhaps Maria and Vi had loaded it with such a hodgepodge to show off the capabilities of the device and not to reveal their own musical tastes.

There was even a Dean Martin song on there, "I Get a Kick Out of You." It was probably one the Dino impersonator in Las Vegas that I had encountered belted out on occasion, although I didn't remember hearing it while I was there.

The more I listened, the more I determined that Maria was right—this was the future of music. The simplicity, convenience, compactness, variety and singular joy of music was all bound in that small contraption. Sure, I was living in the past, musically, but I could see the potential of the device. My huge collection couldn't travel with me, but perhaps a section of it could. I would need Maria to teach me more. Again, musically speaking.

"I WOULD HANG with you tonight but I've got to go cover the Gophers this morning, and tomorrow I'm at the Metrodome. Vikings play the Bucs."

"I'm busy tonight anyway, Freddie."

"Got you a hot date, eh?" he asked.

"No, I'm actually going on a field trip to a music studio," I said. "Going to learn a bit about production and arrangements."

"What for? Sounds boring."

"It's not. And it might be something I want to pursue. It's certainly more appealing than what I've been doing."

"You should forget all that, call Gidget and have some fun."

"Freddie, I'm not interested—"

"Oh, by the way, I have that clipping you wanted. I think."

"Great."

"I'll drop it off on my way to the stadium. I got all your stuff."

"What stuff?"

"The stuff you left behind when you quit the paper. The notepads, clippings, that mug with the picture of the homeless guy..."

"My 'Aqualung' mug! I was wondering where that went."

"Yeah, I saved all that crap for when you came to your senses and returned to the only job you're halfway decent at."

"Freddie, how many times do I have to tell you—"

"Gotta go now. I'll see you in a bit."

I recalled that I had left the reporting job in a rush and hadn't bothered to clean out my desk before landing at La Scala. Freddie had put my old notepads to good use, apparently, pranking new reporters by asking them to decipher my arcane shorthand. He got some entertainment out of those episodes.

With nothing but time on my hands now, I told myself I should go through my spare bedroom and finally sort it out. Boxes of musical finds were now supplemented with cartons of artifacts from my latest gig. I peeked in the room at the profusion of boxes and had second thoughts, however. They weren't going anywhere. Why rush?

I managed to piddle away a few hours doing mundane tasks— washing clothes, vacuuming (long overdue, I might add), cleaning the bathroom, replenishing my near-empty larder. By early afternoon, I had run out of steam and collapsed on the sofa with a beer and the remote to watch an afternoon of gridiron glory.

As the Gophers were just concluding a heartbreaking overtime loss to Purdue, Lena rang.

"How's it feel ta be a free man?" she asked.

"Weird," I said. "I feel like I'm drifting out to sea, and I know there's an island out there somewhere, but I'm not sure where or when I'm going to land on it."

"Any word from Emmie?"

"The last word. It's done. She picked up her final check and she's not coming back."

"Sorry ta hear dat, chief."

"It was too good to be true."

"Aw, now don't feel dat way, Beers. She was inta ya from da get-go. Musta flipped out when...y'know."

"Yeah. Anyway, how's it going down there in New Orleans?"

"Really strange. It's like I nevah left. Seein' da same folks I useta pawty wit' down in da Quawtah."

"And the job."

"A job's a job, Beers. But it's awright. You should come down an' see 'bout workin' heah. Dey need some help!"

"I'm done with department stores," I replied. "I think I need to move in a different direction."

"Well, you oughta come down anyway. You got time on ya hands. Vikings play da Saints next week an' I can get some tickets. Think about it."

"That sounds like fun. I'm not sure where I'll be tomorrow or what I'll be doing, however."

"You know my numbah. Gimme a call."

A road trip down to New Orleans might be a nice segue into my next life, whatever that might be. At least it would be something to do until I figured it out.

55

While I had no preconceived notion that the field trip would lead to a career revelation, I had to go through the motions, play out the string. It was sort of like all the investigations I had undertaken in the past two years—follow a lead, see where it goes.

Of course, I was now being tugged back in the direction of La Scala, with a sudden infatuation with the mysterious and sensual Maria Daventi. My brain told me it was futile, she wouldn't be here long, she was out of my league. Other areas of my anatomy begged to differ.

Freddie dropped off my box of crap at the apartment office downstairs, which was just as well. He didn't have the time and I didn't have the energy to get into another episode of "you know you want to—no, I don't."

There were few revelations in the collection. My "Aqualung" mug was indeed there, but it had a chip on the rim I didn't recall. My Yankees cap was crumpled but still wearable, souvenir of a trip to New York to interview for a Post job I didn't get.

And the clippings were a royal mess, stuffed willy-nilly inside a notebook. The first few pages had neatly cut out and glued down stories, marking my initial days as a cub reporter in Charleston, South Carolina. That quickly devolved into a lazy, haphazard, "ain't got time for this" collection of pages. Well, now there was time but no incentive.

The story was near the top of the heap because it was one of the last I wrote before my departure from journalism. The top of the page featured a rare Twins victory—rare that year, anyway, as they finished 33 games out of first in the division.

And there at the bottom of the page was Jane, in happier times, with her motley crew of jock wannabes. The whole section was intact, so I flipped to the jump and read the rest of my brilliantly clever prose:

continued from Page D1

the chief neurosurgeon for Abbott Northwestern Hospital.

Their official titles mean nothing on this field, however, as they are known by other sobriquets: Overside, Trotter, Rambo, Grammy, Winkie. Even some of the spectators shouting from the sidelines have nicknames—Buff, Footie, Tingler.

Music is blaring at this practice, the sounds of the '70s, the kind of music designed to fuel an up-tempo workout.

At one point, the ball caroms off a player's derriere, triggering an episode of giggling and flopping on the field. That doesn't seem to sit well with at least one spouse on the sidelines, who urges the players to take the game seriously. He constantly gets worked up over mistakes and missed kicks, whereas the players just appear to be having fun—when they aren't doubled over in pain.

"That's the beauty of this league," Milly "Overside" Paulson says. "We try to put all the stress of everyday life on the sidelines while we go out there, run around and have a ball—a soccer ball, that is!"

Meanwhile, Mr. Intensity seems to be melting down at times like the too tightly wound parent of a 10-year-old Little Leaguer. Player-coach Jane says they just laugh it off. "I tell my teammates it's about exercise, camaraderie and unwinding from whatever makes you tense. If you don't come out here to have fun, what's the point?"

"If you don't get a kick out of it, why bother?" says Britnie "Winkie" Culligan.

Winning, which seems to be the goal of the spectator coach, is the last concern of these rocking kickers. "Come on, ladies, let's kick out the jams!" Winkie shouts, urging the players down the field.

They may not beat the Screaming Meemies, but they'll certainly get their kicks.

THE CONCLUSION of the story brought a smile to my face. One of the better acts of journalism I committed at the Herald. Maybe I was really a feature writer and just hadn't been in the right situation. The bulk of my clips were straight game recaps that failed to demonstrate my writing skill.

Not that I was interested in returning to the rag in any form. That ship had sailed and sunk. It was time to open Mystery Door Number Three and see what was behind it.

As I continued basking in the self-congratulatory glow of my hidden talent, I noticed something in the photos on the jump page. It caused me to shiver. I quickly rang Freddie and left a message to call me after the game.

It wasn't long before he returned my call.

"You sound panicked, bud. What's up? You're reconsidering?"

"Nothing like that," I said.

"Because I can—"

"I was looking over the clip of my feature on Jane's soccer team. I need to get in touch with the photographer, Jamey Phelps."

"Dude, you didn't tell me you were out with Merlin on a story."

"Merlin?"

"Jamey, the photog with the knockers."

"Why do you call her Merlin?"

"She had magical tits, man. They would hypnotize you."

"Freddie—"

"I remember one time I had to go out to Vikings training camp and it was hot as blazes. Merlin was shooting that day and she had on a State Fair shirt from when the Herald had that booth. Anyway, she was sweating buckets. It was a wet T-shirt contest."

"Freddie—"

"Always regretted not hooking up with her. Great legs too. She left before I had a chance to tap that."

"Freddie! Can you just find out how I can get in touch with her? Or if I can look at her film from that day?"

"You trying to hook up with her? Cause she's out of your league, bro."

"Would you listen to what I'm saying for once? I need to see the photos she shot that day."

"Oh. Why didn't you say that?" My eyes were rolling to the back of my head. Freddie was so exasperating. "Let me check with the library. They would have filed the shoot."

"OK. It's pretty urgent."

"Dude, chill. I'll get it."

Maybe he would and maybe he wouldn't. Freddie had a way of getting distracted and dropping the ball. There was one other thing I needed to look at. The framed story.

It wasn't anywhere I could find in my apartment. Racking my brain, I figured the only other place it could be was my car. Yep. Still in the trunk.

There was a reason Jane wanted me to have it. My suspicion was confirmed when I removed the back and found a note on the inside.

56

The note was in Jane's handwriting on a piece of La Scala stationery:

> *I had my kicks but it's over. Thank you for showing interest in me at a rough time. We made a connection beyond the confines of the story. I think of you as the son I never had, especially now that there's a further family connection. My tormenter has finally left me alone so I can be at peace in my life. Foot, knee, head, chest, but always keep your hands at rest*

Something clicked. Poring through my Herald box, I located the notepad I had used for the story. The quote was there in my secret shorthand, something I hadn't included in the story. It was the players' mantra, a reminder of the Golden Rule of soccer—you can't use your hands, unless you're a goalie.

I recited it a couple of times. There was something here, something in the note that might lead to the identity of Jane's killer. But what?

My intuition told me it was significant but couldn't tell me exactly why. Thinking back to the other cases I had solved—OK, "solved" isn't quite the term; perhaps tripped over—there was always a musical component. Some of my favorite songs had played a role in the solution to the puzzles I was assigned to unravel.

But no music came. Just silence.

I could put on some music, but would I pick the right tune?

No, it had to be spontaneous. I had to be lightly tripping through the world when a piece of music would assault me, slap me up side the head, wrest its way into my cranium and stake out territory. Therein would lie the answer.

I couldn't go to the music—it had to come to me.

Wait. What the hell was I concerned about it for anymore? Jane was gone. I was no longer involved in the quest to save La Scala and do the job of the police. I was free. Time to start acting like it.

THE FIELD TRIP entailed a visit to the Warehouse District and a recording studio called Center Spin. I was one of four potential students in this class, led by an engineer named Twilly. He didn't say whether that was his first or last name.

While Twilly pointed out features of the control room and the main mixing board, a trio of musicians warmed up in the studio.

"The main board lets you control every channel down to the finest detail. Audio levels, fades, dynamics—it's all there. It may look intimidating, but once you get on it and start moving the dials, you get the feel for it." My fellow classmates looked skeptical. They were probably as clueless as I was about recording. They knew what they liked but wouldn't know how to get there.

Twilly sat at the console and demonstrated as the musicians fired up a song. He narrated as he changed the input levels of drums, guitar and bass to produce different effects. When he asked for a volunteer to engineer the next tune, I stepped forward.

"OK. Our session guys are Rick on guitar—say hi, Rick." The guitar player knocked out a couple of bars of screaming rock, then bowed. "Ben on bass..." The bass player picked out some bottom notes and nodded toward the control room. "George on drums." George pounded the skins for a half-minute before finishing with a cymbal smash and pointing his sticks at us.

"They're going to lay down some tracks and we're going to mix them to get the right sound. You with me?"

I shrugged and said, "Sure."

Twilly sat me at the console, flipped a couple of switches and signaled the players to start. It was somewhere into the second stanza when I realized they were playing a golden oldie, "Kicks," by Paul Revere and the Raiders. It threw me back to an old video I had seen somewhere of the band lip-syncing the tune, with go-go dancers framing the players. It brought a large smile to my face.

When the song ended, Twilly pointed out the pertinent controls, where the channels were stored and what sliders to use in the mixing. Then he said, "Knock yourself out."

The playback started and I waited a couple of measures before working the controls. The drums went down, the bass emerged. I put the guitar through a couple of changes, adding more reverb and boosting the "twang." I was attempting to get it close to the sound of the original, as I recalled it in my dim memory. I let it ride for a bit then tweaked it some more, settling on a groove that pleased my ears.

"That was shit," Twilly commented when the song ended. "Who else wants to try?"

I left the console and told him I was trying to emulate the sound of the original band.

"No one plays that style nowadays and no one wants to hear it anymore," he replied. "This is the 21st Century. We've got all kinds of tools nowadays to produce unique sounds. That's what I'm here to show you."

The next victim sat at the console, the playback began and he started moving levers and dials. The sound jumped erratically from muted to piercing and all levels in between as he constantly fiddled with settings. Twilly just shook his head when it ended.

"Even worse," he said.

The other students, including the only girl in the class, tried their hand at mixing and got the same abrupt dismissal from Twilly. When they finished, he sat at the controls and said he was going to show us how it was done.

The playback began once more. and he moved the dials, shifted the levers and settled on a mellow vibe that sounded like lounge music. The song ended and Twilly smiled up at us. "You see? Not that hard." The other students nodded in agreement, but I thought his interpretation was crap. It was far removed from the intent of the original band and a poor imitation.

"Play that first mix for us again," Rick said from the studio. Twilly looked surprised but complied, and soon my take was wafting through the air, with the musicians nodding to the beat. Rick gave me a thumbs-up when it finished.

There was another exercise, a bit more instruction on the optional tools, then the class was over. I was on the way out the door when Rick caught up to me.

"Liked what you did in there, dude."

"Thanks," I said.

"You know your way around a console pretty well. You do studio work before?"

"No, but I know that song," I replied. "I know how it's supposed to sound."

"Twilly knows theory but he's shit for creativity. We're looking for an engineer for a demo we're putting together. You interested?"

My face started tingling and my heart was pounding. This was a bolt out of the blue, totally unexpected and exciting. Wasn't this what I wanted? A brand new path to the future? I didn't know.

"I don't...I'm not..."

"Consider it an audition," Rick said. "I'll give you my card and you can call me." He patted his pockets and found no card, then told me the band was playing a gig Wednesday at a St. Paul bar. I should come see them and we could discuss it further.

I left with a whole new world of possibilities to intrigue and confuse me.

57

Sunday, September 30

Freddie arrived early to pick me up for the Vikings game against the Bucs. "You're in luck," he announced. "There's a new deputy sports editor coming on board, and I'm pretty sure we'll be able to find you a job."

How many times was Freddie going to try to talk me into returning to sportswriting? He just didn't seem to get the hint that I wasn't interested. I was too tired to fight him yet again so let him ramble on.

The new editor came from a small paper in North Dakota and didn't hold a grudge against me, he explained. The one who was leaving had been my main assignment editor during my stint at the Herald, the one who stuck me with high school club sports assignments, for the most part.

Freddie had met the new fellow briefly Friday, and he seemed like a genuinely nice guy willing to give anyone the benefit of the doubt. Even me. He said his method was to dole out assignments strictly on merit. The better you write, the more prestigious the beat. So I had a good shot at getting a plum job, Freddie said—*if* I could write decently.

I refused to take the bait.

It had been a while since I had attended a game at the Metrodome. There was some sticker shock at the price of beer and snacks, plus an aural assault by too-loud, awful music piped in to get the crowd amped.

"How long have they been doing this?" I asked. "Rap music? Really?"

198

"Hey, it's an entertainment business, a show. Gotta have some show tunes," Freddie replied.

"It's not even music. You can't spell crap without rap."

"Yeah, well you can't spell shit without hit. So what's your point?"

"My point is why don't they play some actual good music over the loudspeakers? There's plenty to choose from."

"Just shut it and watch the game," he said. "I'm working here."

I TRIED TO get into the action but my mind was preoccupied with my own status. As usual, there was more activity inside my noggin than outside. Thoughts swarmed and ran and tackled and eventually got punted. It was introspection football.

A loud groan from the crowd drew my attention back to the field. A player for the Bucs was writhing in agony while players milled around and medical staff attended to him. The replay showed he had taken a hard shot to the left knee, which crumpled at an unnatural angle. I cringed, along with about 60,000 other fans. In time, a cart drove out to pick him up.

The tickle that usually accompanies a revelation of some sort grabbed hold of me. I had no idea what that tingle of electricity signified, or even what it was, but there was something.

Freddie hung around after the game to interview players and write a story, but I had seen enough of that scene. The Crater would be packed with celebrating Vikings fans, also not my scene. So with fewer options—no Emmie to visit, no Dad, not even Lena—I repaired to my humble abode.

TO SAY I was at loose ends would be a huge understatement. There was no imperative impelling me to movement. With all the time in the world on my hands, I didn't know what to do with it. Here I had the opportunity to dive into my music collection for an extended exploration, but it just didn't appeal to me.

There were yard sales, thrift shops, estate sales I could scout, but my hunt-and-gather motivation had been switched off, along with most of my ambition in other areas.

While contemplating how to move forward, I got a call from my sister, Jean. She sounded panicked.

"What the hell is this about Dad moving to Florida?"

"Hi, Jean. How are the kids?"

"You can't let him do that," she continued. "He'll be all by himself down there."

"I hardly think that will be the case."

"You know what I mean," she said. "Who's going to keep an eye on him?"

"He's a big boy," I said. "I think he's doing OK."

"He's old, Jim. He's going to need help that only family can give."

"You make it sound like he has one foot in the grave."

"No, I'm not. But we have a responsibility to take care of him. You can't do that if he's a thousand miles away."

"Jean, you're being melodramatic. He's doing fine. He wants to be around his friends, and he doesn't want to be in the Twin Cities anymore. Because of Jane."

"I'm not moving to Florida," she said.

"I'm not asking you to. He isn't asking you to. He's doing this for himself. Look, it's better for his psyche to get away from here. He'll let us know when he needs something."

"You're not taking this seriously," Jean said.

"I am. Listen, he's an adult. He can decide for himself what he needs to do. He's not an invalid."

"One day he will be."

"OK, then one of us will be there for him. He's fine right now. Just let him live his life."

"You know Tom won't move to Florida." Our older brother lived in Des Moines and was firmly entrenched in his dental practice. It was unlikely he would uproot his family to move near Dad. He had the wherewithal to take our father in when he couldn't live alone anymore, but Dad wouldn't want to move there, I was certain. That left it to Jean or me.

"Who knows, I may move down there," I said. "Just let me get my bearings. Let Dad get his bearings."

"We aren't done with this conversation," Jean said. But apparently we were, because she abruptly hung up on me.

58

It was getting dark when Tina called. Since I had managed to fritter away the rest of the afternoon doing nothing productive, I was open to suggestion. How about dinner? Fine, I said.

We met at a trendy barbecue joint in Dinkytown, a hangout packed with college students. While waiting for our food, Tina asked if I was still serious about leaving the store. I was incredulous.

"How could you think I wasn't serious? I quit. My last day was Friday. I'm not going back," I said.

"OK, I just wanted to make sure."

"You can't talk me out of this, so don't even try."

"I know."

"I'm moving on to the next chapter in my life. Whatever that is."

"Right. Well, the reason I asked...I wanted to get your opinion about something."

"Sure."

"Since you're leaving...left...well, I was thinking about applying for your job."

I was confused at first until I realized she meant head of security, not VP in charge of facilities.

"Super. You would be perfect for that, although..."

"Although?"

"I'm not sure you want the headaches that go with the job."

"Have you seen what I do on a daily basis?" Tina asked. "Let me fill you in. I get to slop mascara and lipstick and rouge and eyeliner and other stuff on heads that would be better off wearing a bag. It's grotesque. There's an occasional pretty girl but for the most part, the cosmetics counter sees the ugly side of humanity. No amount of makeup can fix some of these faces."

"Wow, that's harsh."

"Truth, Beers."

"So you want to escape that and think my old job is the answer."

"I've already done security work, both assisting you and on the police force. I can be tough."

That was an understatement. Although Tina was petite, she was street-wise and capable of fending for herself. I wouldn't want to cross her. If this is what she wanted, who was I to stand in her way?

"You would be great, and I'll be happy to endorse you."

"Could you put in a word with Scalabrino?" she asked.

"No problem," I said. What could he do—fire me? Besides, if Scalabrino really trusted my judgment, like he frequently said he did, he would want my recommendation for a successor. "I'll call him tomorrow."

"Do it now," Tina insisted.

"It's Sunday. I don't think—"

"Do it while you're thinking about it. I want to hear what he says."

Tina put me on the spot. I couldn't say no to her, but disturbing Scalabrino at home on the weekend was probably not conducive to a favorable outcome.

Fortunately, our food arrived and I had a small reprieve while we downed brisket, baby-back ribs, baked beans and corn on the cob, along with a couple of cold longnecks.

After chitchatting about other good eating establishments, we returned to Tina's topic of the evening. She wanted me to phone the mansion as soon as we finished eating. My reticence was no match for her insistence.

I figured I would do a slight end-run and ask for Joe T, thinking it best to go through the proper channels. But when I dialed the number he usually answered, Scalabrino picked up.

"Um, hello, Mr. Scalabrino."

"Mr. Biersovich," he said. "Very fortuitous that you should call. I was about to dispatch Joseph to seek you out."

"Oh?"

"Please come to the mansion as soon as you can."

"What? Sir, I'm not—"

"Call me Johnny."

There was that line again. Always insisting on calling him Johnny. I didn't want to call him Johnny. I didn't want to be his friend. I wanted distance. Permanently.

"Let's go," Tina whispered. She had been eavesdropping and heard the other end of the conversation.

"Are you crazy?"

"Beg pardon?" Scalabrino asked.

"Not you, sir. I'm with…I have a date, you see, and I can't—"

"Bring the young lady with you."

Tina was grinning and nodding. The perfect scenario in her mind, I was certain. But I didn't want to go there ever again.

"I PRESUME you've heard about the latest national horror." Scalabrino was holding court behind his massive desk. Tina and I had been offered drinks but had declined. She was trying to make a good impression; I was keeping my distance.

"I'm not sure what you're talking about, sir." Scalabrino frowned. Joe T stepped up and dropped the front page of the Herald on my lap. "Just below the fold," he said.

There was a story about anthrax being delivered to some businesses in major cities, with threats becoming widespread elsewhere. When I looked up, Scalabrino said, "We've had our threat delivered in the last 24 hours."

Tina snatched the paper from me and read. "Who sent the threat, sir?" she asked.

"Call me Johnny, Miss McEntire," he said. "The mailroom received a suspicious envelope. They alerted the authorities and it is being evaluated. We had to evacuate the executive suite yesterday. Fortunately, not many are working on Saturday."

"+The mailroom?" I asked. It was a place I rarely ventured in my time at La Scala. A dingy room just a few doors down the hall from my original shoebox of an office. The mail clerk was an old guy named Henry Chiselwith, who looked like a character out of a Dickens novel, but much scarier. He didn't have a record, so far as I know, but looked like he could handle a shiv. I rarely had to intersect with him since I got no mail to speak of and never received any packages.

"Mr. Chiselwith indicated that you might know something about it."

59

The insinuation that I knew anything about this anthrax threat stunned me. "Me? Why would I have anything to do with that?"

"Mr. Chiselwith said that was your bailiwick," Scalabrino replied. "Something about you were the expert on the topic."

Then it hit me. He was talking about Anthrax, the '80s band.

"Sir, I think he was spoofing you. Anthrax is a metal group, thrash."

Scalabrino looked at me with puzzlement on his face, then glanced at Joe T, who shrugged.

"It's a rock music group. Has nothing to do with any threat to the store, chemical or otherwise."

"Johnny, why don't you let me find out what I can from my sources inside the police department." All eyes turned to Tina. "I know some people," she added.

Tina gave me a look that told me this was my cue. "Mr. Scalabrino, has Maria left yet?"

"No, but she's eager to move on. I wish you would reconsider."

"I can't, sir. But I can recommend an excellent replacement, somebody with much more skill than myself in the field of store security."

"Oh?" He raised his ample eyebrows. "And who might that be?"

I waved both arms toward Tina, who smiled brightly at the boss.

"Miss McEntire? Oh. I hadn't considered that."

"She would be perfect. She's been right beside me on all these...events at La Scala, even has experience working undercover in the police department. Not to mention her contacts within the force."

Scalabrino considered for a minute. "Yes, Mr. Biersovich. I think you're right. Miss McEntire, what do you think?"

Tina smiled and nodded.

"Why don't you stay for dinner and we can talk about it. The kitchen staff is putting some steaks on the grill and—"

"We've eaten, sir," I said.

"Oh. I see."

"I could probably handle a petite filet," Tina said. Scalabrino smiled at her.

"You don't have to eat if you're not hungry, Mr. Biersovich, but I would like you to stay."

"Thanks, but I really need to get back and take care of a few things. Tina, you coming?"

"I want to stay," she said.

"We'll see that she gets home after," Joe T said.

So I left Tina at the mansion to work on her resume before a live audience. Good for her. I hoped. I didn't want her to find herself in the predicament I had encountered. But Tina was more qualified and tougher overall, so I didn't worry about it much.

On the drive back, Pink Floyd popped up again on the car radio, singing "Time." I let the soothing sound wash over me until I was jerked sideways by the line *Kicking around on a piece of ground in your home town.*

Usually there's a tickle down my spine when I stumble upon a clue that leads me to the solution of a case. This was a bolt of lightning that gave me goose bumps down to the tops of my toes.

I still didn't know what it meant, but I would need Tina once she completed her job interview.

I SPENT the rest of the evening rereading my story and notes, scribbling new notes. There was definitely something here, but I asked myself a couple of times why I was bothering. Wasn't I totally out of the picture? Yes, but...Tina wasn't. I couldn't abandon a friend if I could help.

Before wrapping for the night, I called Freddie and impressed upon him the urgency of my mission. He promised he would come through and spared me the usual job spiel.

The last call of the night was to Lex, who had forgotten about my request. He said he would call me in the morning with the information.

I laid my head on my pillow with the self-assurance that I was going above and beyond the call of duty. But I was doing it for Jane and Tina. And maybe just a bit for Emmie, who was gone from my life but not forgotten.

The dreams came fast and furious. Driving a bus full of convicts around precipitous mountain roads. Sharing an ice cream with a girl from my eighth-grade class whom I hadn't thought about in 20 years. Watching myself watching TV in a dark living room, not my own. Being chased by a man with a pistol into a gun store, where I somehow had the time to shop for a weapon to defend myself.

In the middle of the night, I woke with a start and the clarity of the dreamscapes I had encountered. I was panting, probably from mental exhaustion. As usual, the dreams made little sense.

Although getting a gun seemed like it might be a good idea.

60

Monday, October 1

A new month had arrived and I was glad to see it. September 2001 was a disaster in so many respects. It was absolutely the worst month of my four decades on Earth.

October brought with it my first week of unemployment. I had been continuously employed since I left college in my early 20s. This was a new state of existence, and I didn't know the rules.

My ingrained pattern of waking at 7:00 persisted. I had to ask myself: Why am I up? There was no urgency to eat and shower and get dressed for work. The schedule was blown up. I was free. Well, as free as one can be with no income and no roadmap to same.

Suddenly, I had all the time in the world to work on those chores I had been putting off, the ones I told myself I would handle if I ever had the spare time. Like getting my car tuned up and finally going through all the boxes of unsorted music in the spare bedroom. I was just about to flip a coin to plan my day when I was saved by the bell.

"Hi, is this Jim?" I didn't recognize the voice.

"Yes, Jim Biersovich."

"Hi. This is Jamey Phelps. Fred Skelton asked me to call you."

"Oh, hi, Jamey. Thanks for calling." I was amazed that Freddie had come through so quickly on my request. This was good, though. I could pass her along to Tina and let the new sleuth tackle this line of questioning.

"You need some photos shot? You finally getting married?" she asked.

"No, nothing like that. I just had some questions about an assignment you shot for the Herald."

"I'm not there anymore."

"Yeah, I know. I was just wondering if you had any old photos of a shoot you did a couple of years ago. It was for a feature I did on a soccer team."

"Might have. What was the story?"

I explained as much detail as I could—time, place, date the story ran. Jamey said she didn't have the negatives but was still on good terms with the photo chief and could look them over if necessary. Why did I want to see them?

When I told her it was for a murder investigation, she was enthusiastic. "That sounds a lot more interesting than the bar mitzvah I have to shoot this week. Let me go look for the film and I'll call you back."

Things were looking up. I had a good feeling that Jamey would be able to help me pinpoint clues that would guide Tina. I owed her that much. She had helped me many times when I was the main detective.

TINA CALLED midmorning to report that the anthrax threat turned out to be flour. I could see this scare tactic being deployed frequently to disrupt business. In fact, it threw suspicion back on the owners of Brand X, as Salmon Foster called the enemy store. They would certainly benefit from disruption of commerce at La Scala.

I was sitting in the lobby of the dealership, waiting for the overdue maintenance on my unspectacular but mostly functional vehicle, when a decisive thought struck me. I grabbed my phone. She didn't answer, but I left a message.

In short order, I got a return call.

"Where y'at, Beers? Long time no chat."

"Hey, Lena. Thought I would get you caught up with stuff here and run something by you."

"Shoot, chief."

"I'm officially an ex-employee of La Scala."

"Congrats. Join da club."

"It looks like Tina is going to take over my old job."

"Yeah, spoke wit' her yestahday. She seems excited."

"And I've got lots of time on my hands. Thought I might take a road trip. Down south."

"Heah? Come on down!"

"Can you find me a cheap motel, maybe someplace close to the French Quarter?"

"No way. You stayin' wit' me. Got an apawtment in Fat City, two bedroom. Stay as long as ya like."

"Fat City?"

"Metry. It's da happenin' place."

"Well, thank you. That's perfect."

"When ya comin'?"

"I'm getting my car serviced as we speak. I just need to throw some stuff in a bag and hit the road. I guess it'll take a couple of days to drive down."

"Call me when ya leavin'. I'll stock da kitchen and get ya room ready."

With the car maintenance completed, there was only one thing to do. Start packing before I had second thoughts. There was no reason *not* to go, nothing to keep me in the Twin Cities.

But I didn't escape fast enough.

LEX PHONED as I was zipping up my traveling bag. He said he would forward the suspicious emails he found in Jane's computer. I informed him that I didn't have a computer. No fax either. He said he would read them to me.

The first couple were vague threats from an anonymous sender, along the lines of cut it out, you're pissing me off. The one that caught my attention was bizarre. I made Lex read it back to me so I could write it down:

Sometimes you kick, sometimes you get kicked.
It's interesting when people die. Give us dirty laundry.

The police had no clue what it meant, Lex said. I thanked him and hung up.

The problem was, I *had* a clue.

61

Tina was too busy to talk, understandably so. I decided a visit to the old workplace was in order.

The store was as I recalled it. Of course, it had only been a few days since I had worked there, so there wasn't much time for it to change. Some folks didn't even realize I had quit. I guessed the word hadn't trickled down to the rank and file.

Tina was working in my old office, where Bradley was returning my file cabinet after relocating the computer and phone.

"Dude, you're back!"

"No, Bradley, just visiting."

"You got a gig yet?" he asked.

"Working on it."

"Whatever."

"I thought you were in the watch department."

"They still want me to haul shit around occasionally." He continued wrangling office gear. Tina was engrossed in something on the computer screen, and it took a minute for her to look up.

"Quickly, Beers. I've got a ton of stuff on my plate," she said.

I told her about Jamey's photos and the emails, suggesting she follow up. No can do, she said. Street crew prepping to fill in the hole and return the avenue to some semblance of normalcy. She was ordered to monitor the work, in case a new problem should arise. Just type up some notes, she added.

The computer in front of me was occupied, so I walked down the hall to the executive suite and into Jane's old office. Maria was there, packing things into boxes.

"Hello, Jim. I'm glad you stopped by before I left."

"You're going back to Las Vegas?"

211

"Yes. I've done all I can do here. Foster is working on a replacement."

I had mixed emotions about this development. I was sad to see her leave, because I still had a small notion that we could hook up again. On the other hand, I could understand her desire to exit the Twin Cities and get back to where the action is.

"Close the door." The command surprised me a little, but I complied quickly. Maria drew me to her and held the sides of my face while kissing me. It was a good, long kiss. I had visions of office sex until she pushed me away and said, "Now get out of here and get on with your life."

"But I..."

"We're two ships passing in the night, Beers. We've got other ports to visit. If you're ever in Las Vegas, look me up." She smiled broadly, picked up the box, opened the door and left.

After regaining my composure, I set about the task at hand, setting aside my computer aversion. The lines of inquiry were plentiful, as were the suspects. I listed them and tried to attach a percentage of guilt to each one.

The rival department store chief was at the top of the list. Means, opportunity, motive. It was all there.

Next was the ex-husband. Another high likelihood. Didn't they say most murders are committed by friends or relatives? "They" probably knew what they were talking about. Jane also had an estranged son that could be involved.

I couldn't ignore the terrorist angle. Everyone was still on high alert for danger from strangers. This seemed less likely, however, due to the method of execution.

There were some other unspecified suspects—someone on the construction crew, deranged neighbor, the mystery emailer, perhaps a politician. That last possibility seemed viable since it had played out that way in a previous case.

And there was one other suspect, in-house, that I couldn't shake. It seemed unlikely, but the circumstances made it very suspicious.

I read over my notes, decided it was disjointed but at least a starting point, and hit the print button. When I returned to Tina's office to deliver it, she was leaning back in the chair, staring at the ceiling.

"I typed up anything I could think of," I said, offering her the sheets.

She glanced at them, then spoke. "Beers, what if this is some sort of terrorist plot?"

"I cover that in the notes," I said, holding the pages closer to her. "It seems unlikely, but I guess it's a concern."

"We're not equipped to fight that," Tina said. "There's no way to protect the store from someone crashing a plane into it."

"You're right. But I doubt that's what's going on here. Those guys blow things up, chop off heads—"

"We've seen that before," Tina said soberly.

The vision of Harry Devin's severed head in a box dashed in from the recesses of my memory. I shuddered.

"They don't generally shoot people is what I'm saying. I think this is more mundane than that," I replied.

"Mundane?"

"You know what I mean. Revenge, jealousy, something along those lines."

"You're probably right."

The suspicion that was nagging me had been excluded from my report, but I decided to run it by Tina anyway.

"You might want to look into the Salmon Foster angle, but I'm not sure how to go about it."

"What angle?"

"He was trying to fire Jane around the time she was killed."

"What?!" Tina was flabbergasted.

"It's true. He was edging her out. No idea why. He wouldn't say. Some vague excuse about something she had done in her capacity as head of facilities."

"That may be the smoking gun," Tina said.

"Or it may just be coincidence. Read the notes. I put in some contact information and you can call me. I'll be on the road but—"

"Where are you going?"

"Down to New Orleans. Visiting Lena."

Tina considered that for a minute. "Talk her into coming back. I need her help," she said.

"I don't think—"

"Yeah, I know. Everyone's leaving."

"You don't have to stay here," I offered.

"I do, Beers. This is where I'm from. My people are here. Where would I go?"

I didn't have an answer for that. All I knew was it wasn't the place for me anymore. We hugged, and I departed with a promise to keep in touch and lots of regret.

62

There were a few chores I needed to attend to before hitting the road. First, put a stop on mail. I had to wait in line for a bit at the post office but finally got that sorted out.

Next, clear out the fridge. Didn't want to return home to find The Blob taking over.

Finally, I checked in with the apartment building's office manager and asked her to keep an eye on the place. Didn't know how long.

I was making one last pass through the apartment when Jamey called. She had located the negatives and was ready to look through them with me. Just what I needed to slow down my momentum.

I was reluctant to follow through, but then I thought Freddie would go nuts when I told him I was alone with Jamey in a darkroom. It would be worth it just to see his reaction. Jamey's darkroom was in her house. Even better.

Before my final exit, I snagged an ice chest that I could load with energy drinks for the road. It was a long haul, and I needed to stay alert.

Jamey's place was on a very shady street in West St. Paul. The yard was a bit overgrown but dotted with gazing balls of various sizes and colors. The screened front porch was hung with a trio of wind chimes. I jangled the one nearest the door, then knocked.

"Jim?" Jamey called through the door.

"In the flesh," I said, inadvertently quoting a Roger Waters album title.

"Come on in."

I followed her through a short hall into a side room that must have been an office. It was full of shelves of camera gear, interspersed with large, eye-catching photos, presumably shot by her. She led me through a doorway into a darkroom, closed the door and turned out the light. A red light came on.

"I've got 47 usable frames here. Some are obviously repeats. If you look at this contact sheet..." She handed it to me. "I've marked the unique images and started printing them. If you see something you want me to zoom in on, let me know."

She set to work as I perused the contact sheet and a number of prints already hanging to dry. I recognized Jane right off the bat, even in the odd light, but I was in the dark, literally, on the rest of the team without a key. It was a bit claustrophobic, but at least I wasn't stuck in a 3-by-5-foot room with Freddie.

Jamey worked methodically at pumping out the prints, and soon the entirety of the small space was festooned with images draped from wires crossing the room. Finally, she turned off her enlarger, turned on the light and opened the door.

"Give those a couple more minutes to dry. Glass of wine?" she asked.

"Sure, why not?" More ammunition to fire at Freddie.

We settled onto a couch across from her desk and sipped wine. I noticed that Jamey was nicely put together and had a face with character—a few wrinkle lines but they accented her fabulous smile and deep tan. I probably hadn't noticed her during my stint at the Herald because I had a steady girl at the time.

"You going to tell me about this case?" she asked.

There was no reason to keep it hush-hush anymore, I told myself. No longer on the payroll, no longer on the case. It wasn't a state secret.

I tried to condense it into a Reader's Digest version, leaving out most of the speculation, but focusing on the bits of data that led me to request Jamey's shoot. She appeared impressed.

When she got up to gather the prints, I crossed the room to examine one of the photo murals. It was a picture of a woman and young girl, presumably her daughter. The girl was holding a daisy in both hands, with the woman's arms draped around her. It was a special moment that had a stunning impact. The picture was worth not a mere thousand words, but probably an entire book.

Jamey had talent, and not just the kind Freddie considered worthwhile.

Behind me, she was laying out the photos on a desk, talking as she did so. "These are more or less in order, although I'm grouping the action shots over here and the static shots there. Take a look."

My eyes passed over the rows of pictures, left to right, down, right to left—and then I saw something that stopped me. My heart pounded. I picked up a print.

"Is that something?" Jamey asked. "What do you see?"

"Do you have IDs on the people in this shot?" I asked.

"Let me look," she answered. Jamey grabbed a sheet out of the sleeve that held the negatives. "I've got names on here...it's been a few years...usually I put the notes in with the file...hold on." She put it down and went to retrieve the negatives, holding them up to the light while cross-referencing with her notes.

"Number 13...OK...yeah, 15 and 16..." She ran the negatives through her hand. "Here we go. Frame 29. That's what you have there. And that would be..." She looked at the sheet. "Britnie...Britnie..."

"Culligan," I said.

"Yeah, Culligan That's right. Good memory."

"And this guy here?"

"Let's see...that's... Hunh. No name." She looked at me. "Was he there the whole time? Because if he was, I probably would have talked to him and gotten his name."

"Do you remember someone shouting on the sidelines?"

"No, I don't...wait. Yeah, I do. Was it this guy? He was angry or something."

"Wanted the players to get serious, not clown around on the field."

"Right. Now I remember. 'Kick 'em when they're up, kick 'em when they're down.'"

A shudder ran through me. "What did you say?"

"'Kick 'em when they're up, kick 'em when they're down.' That's what this guy yelled at one point. Don't know why that stuck with me."

"Jamey, you are fabulous." I grabbed her, kissed her full on the lips and scooted out before she could ask me any more questions. I didn't have time for that. Just time enough for one more errand before hitting the road.

63

I couldn't get near the store. Work crews had completely shut down Hennepin, so I parked two blocks away and walked.

Huge backhoes, paving machines and asphalt trucks were making their way across the former chasm, reverting it to usable roadway. Spectators lined both sides of the street behind barricades, and a lineup of idle workers observed inside the perimeter.

I scanned the crowd for a certain person that I knew would be in attendance. When I found the man in question, I was shocked to see him in animated conversation with Tina.

Before I could head that way, a voice at my left shoulder said, "I thought you ran away." I turned to see Detective Farraday glaring at me.

"My friend is in danger," I said, pointing across the street. He looked in the direction I was indicating, then frowned at me.

"She's safely out of the way."

"I don't mean the trucks. That guy—" I signaled the man standing next to Tina. "He's the killer."

Farraday smiled. "Sure he is." He turned to go.

"Wait! I can prove it. But you need to get him away from Tina. He's murdered at least two store employees." Farraday considered me again, saw I was serious, then waved at a couple of officers at the edge of the crowd. He ordered them across the street to chat with the man in question.

The next series of events happened in a matter of seconds, although the action seemed like it was in super-slow-motion to me.

As officers made their way across the street, the man spotted them and quickly grabbed Tina around the throat with his forearm.

He was reaching into a pocket for something when one of the idle workers swung a shovel and bashed him on the back of the head. He went down in a heap, carrying Tina with him.

The officers sped to the site and I wasn't far behind. A crowd was forming around the scene but I pushed my way through behind the policemen. I heard someone mutter "Dumb sumbitch" as I broke through the cordon. The police officers had already flipped the man onto his stomach and were applying handcuffs. Someone was helping Tina to her feet.

"Are you OK?" I asked her.

"Yeah, I'm fine," she said. "What the hell was that?"

"Sir, you'll have to step back," an officer told me. Police were pushing the crowd back as they escorted the man to a nearby cruiser. One invited Tina to ride downtown and give a statement.

When I turned, Farraday was again at my elbow. He extended the same invitation to me.

TWO HOURS LATER, Tina and I were dismissed with the understanding that we would be called to testify when the case went to trial. For her part, Tina was too shaken to return to work, so I offered to buy her a drink. I was still hoping to make a getaway, but it was getting late. My departure looked like it would be delayed a day.

Sam delivered a couple of frosty mugs, and Tina requested a shot of bourbon on the side. Her hand was only a little shaky as she lifted her beer. I hadn't even begun to fill in the details when a familiar face appeared at the door of The Crater.

"They told me you might be over here," Joe T said upon arrival at our table. "Drinking on company time?"

"I'm not," I replied. "And Tina needs it after what she went through."

Joe T looked at her, then back at me. "Mr. S would like to invite you to the mansion for a little tête-à-tête."

"Go see Detective Farraday," I said. "He has all the information you need. I'm on my way out of town."

Joe T just stared at me.

"C'mon, Beers," Tina said. "Too late to go anywhere today. You would barely make it to Iowa before dark."

She had a point.

"I'll make sure the kitchen staff prepares something. And you won't have to drink on your own dime," Joe T said. "I'll even be the designated driver."

Another offer I couldn't refuse.

64

The rowing machine was at the curb when we pulled up into the circle in front of the mansion.

"What's the deal—"

"Don't ask," Joe T cut me off.

Inside, Scalabrino was perched behind his battleship-size desk with his beefy hand around a highball glass.

"So good of you to come, Mr. Biersovich. Miss McEntire, may we fix you a drink?"

Tina ordered a straight shot of whiskey to calm her nerves. I didn't have that problem so I opted for another beer. Joe T did the honors, and we settled into the big leather chairs facing desk. Scalabrino gave his usual command: "Report."

"In a nutshell, the killer has been apprehended," I said.

"This we know," Scalabrino replied. "Expound."

I looked toward Tina. "This is your show now. You want to do the honors?"

She shook her head. "You know more than I do."

So I expounded, starting with the proximity to 9/11 and the fear that terrorism had spilled into La Scala. I detailed the distractions of security camera installation, health inspection shutdown and the ouster of Jane Mertin orchestrated by Salmon Foster.

Then I focused on the various problems presented by street construction, not least of which was the damage to the subbasement wall and subsequent flooding, which led to the discovery of the dead clerk.

"For awhile, I thought the enemy store was directing all the onslaughts. It looked like the perfect scenario to cripple your business."

"You have no idea, Mr. Biersovich. This is constantly going on behind the scenes. Mr. D— is relentless."

"That seems obvious. It seems fairly certain he had a hand in siccing the health inspector on you."

"No doubt."

"What about the ex-husband?" Joe T asked.

"I ruled him out fairly quickly. Besides the fact that he was a thousand miles away when Jane was murdered, the clues pointed elsewhere."

"Didn't you find something about some strange phone calls?" Tina asked.

"Yeah. Jane apparently made calls to a restaurant in California. Turns out her older son, the one she was estranged from, worked there. She was trying to make peace with him."

"He has a record, I understand," Scalabrino said.

"A drug conviction," I explained. "But again, no real motive to kill Jane, and he was also a thousand miles away at the time."

"So where did the clues point?" Joe T asked.

"The soccer team," I said. Eyebrows went up all around. I briefly outlined my invitation to work at La Scala following the feature on Jane's over-40 soccer league. Scalabrino had never heard that story before and expressed surprise.

"So you really had no security experience?" he asked.

"I told you that a thousand times."

"Yes, but I thought you were just being modest," Scalabrino replied. "We'll need to revisit our hiring practices, Joseph." Joe T nodded.

"Anyway, Jane's son, Lex, helped me figure this out."

"I thought you said he wasn't around?"

"Her younger son. He came in for the funeral and found some things that pointed to a soccer connection."

"Like what?" Scalabrino asked.

"Jane had a framed copy of the story I wrote in her kitchen. Lex was going through her things and saw a note she wrote on the back, saying to give it to me.

"It only had the first page of the story, not the jump. Inside the frame was a cryptic note from Jane, indicating someone was harassing her. Also, she had written a chant the players used at practice."

"Chant?" Joe T asked.

" '*Foot, knee, head, chest, but always keep your hands at rest.*' "

"What does that mean?" Tina asked.

"It's a soccer thing. You can kick the ball or propel it with your head or chest, but only the goalie is allowed to handle it."

"How is that pertinent?" Scalabrino asked.

"The two murders at La Scala. I checked the autopsy reports. Jane was killed with a shot to the chest, but she was also shot in the foot. The clerk was shot in the head and the knee."

"Seems coincidental," Joe T remarked.

"Not in light of the other clues. Jane had also received some odd emails, one of which seemed to tie it together. It was a lyric from 'Dirty Laundry': *It's interesting when people die. Give us dirty laundry.*"

"The pertinence escapes me. Elaborate," Scalabrino commented.

"The killer quoted the same song at soccer practice."

"And you remember this because…?"

"I didn't remember it. But the photographer did. I looked up the woman who shot the photos for the story. She went through her film and found photos of the guy on the sidelines. She remembered him shouting: 'Kick 'em when they're up, kick 'em when they're down.' Which is from the same Don Henley song."

"I think I need another drink," Tina said. She was apparently still shaken by the notion that the killer had an arm around her throat.

I concurred and asked for another beer.

65

A phone call interrupted my debriefing. It was from Farraday, asking Scalabrino to come to the police station at his convenience. He indicated he would be there in the morning. I continued with my recitation.

"The man had some sort of soccer background. I had Lena do some research, and she found out he was on an elite soccer team and tried out for the Olympics. In addition, he had romantic links to some of the players."

Scalabrino scowled at me. "Explain."

"Jane dated him for awhile, apparently. I don't know any details, but it seems obvious they had some sort of relationship. She hinted at it in her note. Also, and I'm not certain of this, I suspect he had an affair with the deceased clerk."

"Holy shit," Tina said.

"You have evidence of this?" Joe T asked.

"Not as such. But all signs point to that. The kicker, so to speak, was the photo shoot. Also, this guy was the foreman on the street project. I met him in his trailer one day. Believe it or not, his nickname is Footie."

"So there was no sinister plot, either from terrorists or competing businesses," Scalabrino summarized.

"Nope. Appears to be a simple case of jealousy, rage, what have you. The dead clerk was stealing from the register so she could buy a gun to protect herself."

"You didn't tell me that," Joe T said.

"I thought I did. Anyway, that's what her co-workers intimated. There were other clues, like the deflated soccer ball found in the lower level. I tried to figure out who would have access to the store after hours, or before hours, to stage Jane's body like that. If he was dating Jane, he probably had opportunity to duplicate her keys."

"Another security hole to plug," Scalabrino said, nodding at Tina.

"Sir, I don't know how you can protect the store in all instances from some nut bent on revenge," I said. "You would have to make it an armed fortress, a Fort Knox."

"If need be, that's what we'll do. The safety of our staff is paramount. And the customers, of course."

"There was one other indication that the murders were soccer related. Holly, the clerk in bedding, was out for a time. Come to find out she was shot by an intruder. Holly was the goalie on the soccer squad."

"Another murder?" Tina asked.

"Not murder. She was shot in the hand."

"This guy is indeed a wacko," Joe T commented.

"Way beyond soccer hooligan," I added.

"So once again you have solved a case for me," Scalabrino said. "I am still holding out hope that you will reconsider…"

"Won't happen. Tina will be far more effective than me in the security realm. Trust me." Tina smiled at me.

"What will you do now?" Joe T asked.

I set my glass down and rose from the leather chair. "Take you up on that taxi offer."

Epilog

With only a few hours of worthwhile sleep, I rose before dawn and hit the road. Adventure awaited in the Crescent City.

At midmorning, I called Freddie and reported my whereabouts. Predictably, he wanted to join me on my road trip. When I related my Jamey episode, including our darkroom intimacy and a full-on smooch, he was flabbergasted. I let him think something had happened beyond the routine facts.

"When are you coming back?" he asked.

"Don't know. Maybe a week, maybe a month. Playing it by ear."

"Who am I going to The Crater with? You can't just leave me in the lurch like this."

"Freddie, you'll survive. Make a new friend. There's probably a coed in the Twin Cities you haven't hit on yet."

"Very funny."

"I have to get away, recharge my batteries, think about what I'm going to do next."

"You know—"

"Don't say it. Just don't. I plan on a future remarkably free of newspaper employment. I have no idea what it will be, but it won't be at the Herald. You can count on that."

"Well, why didn't you say so a long time ago?"

It was no use. Freddie remained clueless to my not-so-subtle hints. It's a wonder he was able to function in the modern world at all. I promised to call occasionally to update him on my visit with Lena.

SO MY EMPLOYMENT at La Scala had come full circle. It began with a story about Jane Mertin and her soccer club. Unfortunately, it also ended with the same, under tragic circumstances.

As I tooled down the interstate toward Missouri, an old Nitty Gritty Dirt Band song wafted into my cranium: "Will the Circle Be Unbroken?"

In this instance, it was very broken. Irreparably.

I headed into a future that was unknown, a mine field of question marks. But somehow I knew there would always be music.

♫

This is where I thank all the "little people" that contributed to the continuation of the misadventures of Jim "Beers" Biersovich.

In my mind, they are not little. First and foremost is my superb editor, Dana Davis. I've already extolled her virtues many times in previous installments, so I won't expound too much here, except to say thank you, dear. I wish I had half your knowledge of the English language. Your cheeseburger is in the mail.

I have to thank my small but enthusiastic corps of readers who enjoy these novels. Your encouragement keeps me going at times. Now, if each of you would purchase 10,000 copies, I'd get somewhere.

My grandkids are an excellent source of unending humor. Thank you, Olivia, Genevieve, Gina Marie and Michael for being the hilarious, intelligent youngsters you are.

Of course, my muse, Jeanne Anne, is always there by my side, providing the support and "Lucy" moments that inspire me.

See you in the next installment.

Discover the roots of the Jim Biersovich story. *First Case of Beers*, the initial title in the series, introduces Beers, Lena, Tina, Freddie and the rest of the wacky crew trying to keep the ship of commerce La Scala afloat.

It's Christmas season at the turn of the Millennium. A vandal is causing mayhem in the department store where Beers is head of security.

Although he's not really qualified—his training was as a sportswriter—Beers is charged with finding out who is assaulting Johnny Scalabrino's business. A cryptic clue left at the scene of each incident baffles the amateur sleuth. In the end, his knowledge of classic rock music reveals the key to nabbing the culprits.

First Case of Beers, second edition, was published by Liquid Rabbit Publishing in 2020. It is available from Amazon and BarnesAndNoble.com.

Bet on Beers follows the crew to Las Vegas, where priceless artifacts, including a jade bathtub, have gone missing at the casino store owned by Johnny Scalabrino. Once again, Beers and company are called on to find the perpetrators while navigating the dangerous, high-stakes world of gambling.

This time, murder is on the agenda, and Beers suspects he is out of his league. The heists seem impossible, particularly the theft of the bathtub. A parallel assault on the casino's gambling operation complicates the investigation. Once again, a musical solution presents itself and Beers is able to answer the riddle of this baffling case.

Bet on Beers, second edition, was published by Liquid Rabbit Publishing in 2020. It is available from Amazon and BarnesAndNoble.com.

When the head of a sportswriter, a former co-worker at the Minnesota Herald, appears in the store, Beers discovers a long list of suspects. Everyone wanted Harry Devin dead, or so it seems.

Beers Ahead follows the brain trust through a macabre investigation that lends an even creepier vibe to the Halloween season. Complications distract Beers from his task—mainly oversight of a construction project and a new honey to woo.

A mysterious stranger, a secret correspondent, a vintage chapeau and an unpublished manuscript are some of the elements the team encounters as the complex scheme unfolds. But Beers always has music to guide him down the right path.

Beers Ahead was released by Liquid Rabbit Publishing in 2018. It is available from Amazon and BarnesAndNoble.com.

Jim Biersovich is sent overseas on what figures to be an easy assignment: scout locations in London for a future La Scala department store. But nothing is ever simple for our amateur detective, as he soon discovers in *Beers Abroad*.

With his unofficial assistant, Lena, along for research duties, Beers soon encounters issues with the preferred location. Not only is there an issue with the owners, but also with the security of the site, as murder soon comes into play. Repeatedly.

As the bodies pile up, Beers is dispatched to investigate the owners' reluctance to sell. The disappearance of one of the key figures complicates the negotiations. In the midst of the dilemma, Beers' reporter buddy Freddie arrives on a working junket, throwing more chaos into the mix.

Beers once again is called on to muster his cunning and intuition, along with a bit of help from his friends, to solve the case.

Beers Abroad was released by Liquid Rabbit Publishing in 2019. It is available from Amazon and BarnesAndNoble.com.

The tragedy of 9/11 turns the world upside down for department store security chief Jim Biersovich in *Beers Tapped Out*. In addition to a host of new safety considerations, Beers is confronted with a murder in store and assaults on the business from every angle.

Store owner Johnny Scalabrino is forced to reassess both his lifestyle and store policies to cope with the new reality. Hidden foes are attempting to sabotage his business, compelling him to pull out all stops in an effort to protect his livelihood.

A street project in front of the store creates ongoing mayhem: traffic snarls, flooding and an infusion of pests caused by a construction mishap. Caught in the center of the maelstrom, as usual, is Beers, who faces his own life crisis. Not only is he commanded to solve the murder, he must also solve the enigma of his girlfriend, Emmie, who flees in fright. Is this the end of their relationship? In fact, is this the final straw for Beers, his exit strategy from La Scala?

Beers Tapped Out was released by Liquid Rabbit Publishing in Fall 2020. It is available in paperback and e-book from Amazon and BarnesAndNoble.com.

Coming in Fall 2021:

Beers' world has been turned upside down by the events of the last case. Not only is he single again, but he also finds himself adrift in a new environment.

No longer an employee of La Scala, Jim Biersovich finds a job in the music field, as a late-night deejay for a blues station in New Orleans, where his friend Lena now resides. In *Bayou Beers*, he strikes up a friendship with another deejay and part-time musician, Phineas Stoke.

When Phineas is murdered, Beers finds himself thrust into the middle of another investigation, this time fueled by his own desire to see justice done and assist the family. As he soon discovers, the process of playing detective is complex and exhausting, with roadblocks to navigate and more than a few viable suspects.

Beers enlists the aid of some trusted friends and hangs a shingle, formalizing what he had been doing for the past couple of years. Beers Detective Agency is born. Work starts flowing in, but the main job is learning the identity of his friend's killer.

Bayou Beers will be released by Liquid Rabbit Publishing in Fall 2021.

Follow PM LaRose on Facebook. More information on Jim Biersovich can be discovered at the Beers Detective Agency on Facebook.

Made in the USA
Monee, IL
09 December 2020